Alyn Yates Keith

A Hilltop Summer

Alyn Yates Keith

A Hilltop Summer

ISBN/EAN: 9783337326296

Printed in Europe, USA, Canada, Australia, Japan

Cover: Foto ©Andreas Hilbeck / pixelio.de

More available books at **www.hansebooks.com**

A HILLTOP SUMMER

BY

ALYN YATES KEITH

AUTHOR OF "A SPINSTER'S LEAFLETS"

LEE AND SHEPARD PUBLISHERS
10 MILK STREET
BOSTON

A Hilltop Summer

Electrotyped by C. J. Peters & Son.

TO

M. J. M.

CONTENTS.

A HILLTOP SUMMER

I

RACHEL AND JESSE

WE followed the little procession to the door of the gray old meeting-house, and lingered to watch its slow winding down the hill. Four white-haired men bore the coffin on their shoulders, treading after the old minister with uneven steps. The road was rough, and the mourners jostled each other as they picked their way among the stones. But Aunt Rachel was past being disturbed by any lack of harmony among her followers. The coffin-plate said she had fulfilled her ninety years; but remembering the majesty of the face from which kindly Death had smoothed all lines of age and sorrow, it was hard to believe the legend we had just read while the body lay in homely, solemn state below the high pulpit.

Aunt Rachel did not belong to us ; and, though any one was welcome to join the wavering line that went noiselessly down the sharp hill and turned to the little burying-ground at the right, we sat on the rocks back of the church, listening to the birds that hopped and chirped around us.

It seemed a thing impossible that Death could be, in this living sunshine above the new grass, with the full song of the nesting robins shaking the sweet air.

The cracked bell in the steeple ceased its melancholy stroke as the last of the broken line entered the gate : and the tones of the preacher's voice floated up to us. jarring somewhat upon the peaceful air. There were no tears shed as the coffin was slowly lowered into the grave ; and when the prayer was ended three old men with two old wives and one old daughter turned away with an air of relief. The neighbors shook hands with them in a listless way ; then came briskly up the hill, stopping for a moment at the still open church-door to ask after the health of absent families and the prospect of crops. No one said good-by, but after lingering awkwardly for a while the men slunk away first, and the women followed ; the younger ones dropping back to ask for some new cake receipt, or the best way to dye faded merino.

One old man stayed behind. He stepped cautiously along the uneven rocks, leaning on a heavy staff, and shaded his eyes with one hand as he looked over us to the fresh mound below.

" Well, I'm mighty sorry Aunt Rachel's gone," he said, addressing us with the indifference of age. " She was a proper good woman. Not a child her ekal amongst 'em all, not a one that could hold a candle to Rachel. Mebbe you two didn't know her. No? What a pity! Well, she wa'n't much older'n I be, and I can't think of a time when I didn't know her. Purty girl an' woman as ever you see. Didn't look it, did she? Set down? Well, no, 'bleeged to ye; I've got rheumatics bad, an' 'tain't easy to git up ag'in. Where was I? Oh! Her folks was Babtists, and they kep' her strict, I tell ye. She was babtized one awful cold Sunday over there in the big pond jest beyond the buryin'-ground. She wa'n't more'n sixteen year old, an' jest as purty as a pink — all red an' white; looked jest 's if somebody'd spatted her side o' the face. She went down into the water with the parson; an' when he put her under an' fetched her up ag'in. I shouted Hallelujah as loud as any of 'em. Did it hurt her any, you say? Land sakes, no! Folks never catches cold them times.

"Our Jesse, he stood back with the crowd, and when

she come out all drippin' and solemn, seemed 's if she looked for him fust one. But he turned his head 'tother way an' walked off. I can see him as plain. What for? Why, you see he wa'n't a professor. He didn't b'lieve that way. An' her folks was terrible strict. He was a peart one, if I do say it. An' he was my brother, too. Folks don't allays hev a call to flatter their own, but I ain't no believer in runnin' down your kith an' kin for perliteness to other folks. They couldn't say a word against Jess. Square up an' down he was 'bout everything, an' a mind of his own. He hed a mighty masterful way with him, too; an' pa an' ma they jest hoped he'd get Rachel if he'd wait long enough. Mebbe they thought the old folks 'd die. But old folks will hang on amazin'. An' after a spell he got the Western fever bad, an' nothin' 'd do but to try farmin' on't out there.

"Folks didn't write letters much them days. It cost twenty-five cents to get one, an' money didn't grow onto every bush, way it does now. But Jesse wrote to ma that fall — 'twas spring when he left — an' he sent some word to Rachel. Ma cried, I remember, an' I wondered what for, but she wouldn't tell. It was a Sunday mornin', an' one o' the neighbors fetched her the letter to church. He said he tucked it under the wagon seat when he went to the post-office, an' forgot it for about a week. She carried that letter 'round in her pocket an' never showed it, an' pa said he couldn't get it out of her what 'twas all about. Jess was like ma; straight as an arrer, an' true as preachin', an' mighty close-mouthed.

"After that Rachel didn't come to our house, nor we didn't go there. That winter ma got another letter, an' some on't she read to us, but not all. She waited till meetin' was out to see Rachel, an' said somethin' or 'nother to her. I couldn't make out what 'twas, but the girl redded up an' acted jest's if she'd got somethin' to say, only the deacon was close by, lookin' at her, an' she shet her mouth tight. The deacon, I forgot to say, was her pa.

"Well, 'twas nigh onto five year 'fore Rachel married, an' we'd kind o' lost sight o' Jess. What made her marry? Laws! how sh'd I know? Mark was a good farmer, an' he'd got money laid up. He was a professor, too. He went down into the water that same day with Rachel — buried in babtism, you know; an' we Babtists make a good deal o' that. He wa'n't much of a man after all; sort o' chips in porridge, you know; never did a mite o' harm, but he didn't amount to a row o' shucks. Only he could make money. They used to say he'd pinch a dollar till the eagle on't squealed. When the ol' folks died he got the farm, bein' the oldest, an' I guess Rachel had easier times. For Mark's folks was plaguey hard to got along with. They was all money-makers, tight as a drum. I tell you the ol' man squeezed the pennies!

"An' Rachel had a lot o' children. There was Joe
an' Tim an' Zeke — all jest like their pa.   Then she
had one little girl that took arter her; a purty cretur,
with a smile for everybody; allays givin' away everything she'd got, jest like her ma, the ol' folks said.
She was a lovin' little thing as ever I see, an' Rachel
set store by her.   Mark said she spiled her, but 'twa'n't
so.   She wa'n't that sort.   It's weak stuff that spiles
easy.

"One day they had a sewin'-meetin' to the house, an'
Rachel was awful busy gettin' supper.   'Twas a hot
day, an' the little un played outside.   Jest as they was
all settin' down to the table she come mopin' along in,
an' said her head ached, an' cried some.   Rachel was
that worried, but the minister's wife was there, an' they
all thought she babied the little girl too much: so
Rachel jest told her to run along out an' she should
have her supper when they got through.   She told me
after 'twas all over, seemed 's if 'twould kill her sendin'
the child away so.   Somethin' seemed hangin' over her;
only she was 'shamed to act foolish.   Well, that night
little Mary died sudden: out of her head an' never
knew her mother.   That's her little grave-stone, leanin'
onto one side, over there by Mark's folks — most covered up with grass.   After she was buried Rachel had
a fit o' sickness, an' there wa'n't a mite o' color in her
face when she got over it.

"I reckon 'twas a good thing for her when the old

folks passed away. She didn't have a real easy time
with 'em, bringin' up her boys. Boys will be boys, an'
they didn't like to hev so many orderin' 'em 'round.
Tim, he run away: but when his granther died he got
back ag'in. They was stiddy enough boys, as boys
goes, but they didn't amount to much. Kind o' small
potatoes, every one of 'em. Rachel, she had the snap.
She'd do more work days an' then set up nights with
sick folks than anybody within ten miles o' here. Jest
about a year after Mary died she hed another girl baby,
and by an' by two more boys.

"When Tom — he was the baby then — was big
enough to run 'round, all of a sudden Jess come home.
Pa hed been dead a good many years, an' ma was livin'
with us. Mebbe you don't wan' to hear all about this.
You do, eh? Well, our folks says you can't stop me
when I get onto old times, more'n you could stop a
ox-team runnin' down meetin'-us hill. Where be I?
Oh — yes — I sort o' wondered what Jess'd say, but
my wife she told me to keep still. Jess was a grand
lookin' man, if I do say it. He'd got a big farm out
West, and he said ma must go an' keep house for him.
She was as tickled about it as missy with a new beau;
an' proud! — proud wa'n't no name for it!

"Well, next mornin' I hed to be down medder
turnin' the grass, an' Rachel's little feller was t'other
side the fence hollerin' at me. I was 'fraid he'd get
lost or somethin'd happen to him, so I told him his ma

wanted him, an' purty soon down she come ; for Rachel
never could let one on 'em out of her sight. An' when
I looked 'round, what should I see but Jess comin'
down the lane! I got out o' the way, for it scairt me
to think o' seein' them two together ag'in. Rachel did
a poor thing when she took Mark, for all his money.
It didn't do her a mite o' good, an' his stingy ways was
powerful pinchin' for anybody to put up with, let alone
a big-hearted woman like her, allays helpin' poor folks
an' gettin' scolded for 't, an' bearin' the brunt of everything. Well, I jest scrooched down behind a rock that
I'd allays hated to hev in the medder, but I was powerful glad on 't that day ; an' Rachel picked up her baby
an' started to go back. When she see Jess standin'
still before her, a great, big feller, all dressed up fine 's
a fiddle, she sort o' sunk right down on to the grass.
They didn't shake hands, nor so much as pass the time
o' day. But Jess picked up the little feller, an' set
down, with 'im on one knee, an' took out a big watch
from his wesket pocket for 'im to play with. Rachel
was white as a sheet, an' she didn't seem to open her
mouth : leastways I couldn't hear a word. The little
chap was terrible sassy with 'im, pullin' his whiskers,
and climbin' all over 'im, an' flingin' the watch fur as
'twould go to the end o' the chain. Purty soon Jess
spoke up, an' says he :

  " 'This little feller had ought to be 'n mine, Rachel.'

  " An' then I see Rachel get up like an old woman an'

reach out for the child; but he wouldn't leave Jess.
She put both hands up over her face, an' Jess, he
pushed the boy out'n his lap an' was over the fence an'
up the lane in the shake of a lamb's tail. He went out
West ag'in in a day or two, an' took ma with 'im; 'twas
like bein' set right down in a butter-tub, as we say, an'
there she stayed, rollin' in luxury, she wrote to us, till
she died.

" Now, mebbe you think 'tain't much of a story, this,
but there's a little more to it. By an' by the boys got
along up to be men, narrer, like their pa; scrimpin' in
their ways, so's nobody could get along with 'em unless
'twas their wives. Women folks does have a way of
puttin' up with things that 'd rile a saint. Then Mark
up and died — 'twas one hot summer in hayin' time —
an' Joe got the farm. Rachel stayed on with 'em, an'
did the heavy work. Joe's wife had narves, an' she
couldn't have the babies sleep with her nights; so
Rachel took 'em, and did most o' the bringin' up.
She got enough to eat an' to wear, but 'twas all purty
plain, even for plain folks like us. Someways she managed to look diff'rent from other women folks, even
when she got old an' wrinkled. There was a 'mazin'
peaceful kind o' look on her face, as if this world wa'n't
all there was of it, that I declare to goodness when she
come into church with two or three little uns hangin'
onto her, she was han'some as a pictur'. When any o'
the neighbors took sick, they sent for her, day or night:

an' my wife she says the sight of her face was better'n a dose o' medicine any time.

" Well, it went on that way till she was nigh onto seventy year old. An' then Jess come back ag'in. We was that proud on him! A better lookin' man, an' a younger, for one that was gettin' along, you couldn't pick out in a week o' Sundays. Held his head up 's if 'twas check-reined, high collar, good necktie week days an' all, not a wrinkle in the back of his coat, trousers gallussed up to the right notch, boots shiny. It jes' did your heart good to look at 'im.

" 'Twas Saturday night when he come, an' Sunday we took 'im to church with us. I brushed up some, an' wife she fixed up her bunnit with a new ribbin. Rachel was there in her weeds, with Joe an' his children. Their ma couldn't stan' Babtist preachin' no way : an' she was most giner'ly on her back Sundays. An' Jess, he never took his eyes off'n Rachel. But she didn't see 'm I say, though wife she says she did. What made her think so was because Rachel's cheeks was as pink as peaches. But 'twas a hot Sunday, an' the parson hed a miled-long sermon, about bein' buried in babtism, provin' that the' wa'n't no other way to be saved skercely. My wife, she thought 'twas all gospel truth; an' mebbe I should too if it hadn't been that Jess was settin' right there hearin' of it too.

" When we went home out o' sight o' him an' the neighbors, she nudged me sudden, an' says she :

" ' What d'ye think's goin' to happen ? '

" An' I says, 'Dunno, unless you women folks 've been gittin' up another donation visit to take the bread out o' our mouths.' We'd jest hed one along towards spring; an' I wa'n't the only man that growled some because the parson lived so high without workin' for't like the rest on us.

" Well, she's a master-hand to guess out things, my wife is, an' she tried to get me into 't. I was jest beat out with the heat an' the preachin' and says I, 'Out with it if you've got anythin' to say, an' don't keep me on tenter hooks no longer.'

" But she waited till I'd onlocked the kitchen door, an' then she stepped inside right afore me, an' says she : —

" ' Rachel's goin' to marry Jess this time!'

" I declar' for 't, you could hev knocked me down with a broom splinter! 'You don't say so!' says I. An' I couldn't eat any dinner — leastways not much, an' she hed an extry one that day.

" When Jess come in — he'd been talkin' with Square 'Lias out by the shed — I was goin' to ask 'im. But wife jest hushed me up, an' begun to talk about the weather; an' when we was alone, me an' him, I hedn't got the courage. If I hed, I'd a known ; an' 'twould be a comfort. But that's the end to a long story, an' I reckon you're purty well tuckered out with my talk by this time. Didn't he marry her after all? Well, I'm bound to say, no. He hung round a spell, which wa'n't like Jess, an' use' to go to the house purty often, till Joe as good's invited him to leave. Joe never wasted time l'arnin' manners, from what I heerd say. He told the Square after meetin' next Sunday, that any man that couldn't take care of his own mother hedn't never ough' to hev one.

" I ruther guess they kind o' over-persuaded Aunt Rachel, an' talked about her dooty, an' the foolishness of it all. Jess hed the same old masterful way that most folks couldn't git 'round. But they argied that old folks better be satisfied as they was. An' they got the parson to come down to the house an' tell 'im. It was kind o' town talk for a spell. An' then Jess he went West ag'in, an' said nothin' to nobody; an' not a word have we heerd from that day to this."

The old man walked off, leaning hard on his staff, but turned by the meeting-house steps to set his hat well on the back of his head, and say, " Good day, an' good luck to ye."

One evening just at sunset, we strolled down to the little burying-ground, drawn irresistibly toward the grave of everybody's Aunt Rachel. The robins were piping their happy good-night song, and the world seemed brimful and running over with life and hope. Picking our way among the slanting headstones, we came suddenly upon the new-made grave. Kneeling

beside it was a tall figure with silvery hair. One thin
hand rested on the mound, supporting the body which
had half fallen across it.

Three days later we stood with our old friend beside
another new-made grave, side by side with Rachel's.
The neighbors had left us alone, and the old man
thought aloud, as if we too were gone.

"Jess, my boy, 'twas a hard row you hed to hoe — a
hard row. They
might 've let you
hed her. 'Twa'n't
right. She'd ough'
to hev hed your
prop'ty — not us.
They 'd a buried
you over there in
the swamp corner
if I hedn't hed my
say. They can't
send you away

now, Jess, if you ain't a perfessor. An' whose shall
she be in the resurrection? If the Scriptur's true that
says there they neither marry nor are given in marriage, but are as the angels of God, I don't see
why you ain't got jest as good a claim to Rachel as
Mark hed. For lovin's the main thing up ther, I
reckon, Jess, my boy, an' you've allays loved her
dear."

II

JESS'S MONEY

WE came to Hilltop when the trees were just beginning to thicken at their twigs. The little runways that

slid down the hills carried a faint line of growth along their edges, as if tidy Nature had turned over a green hem of earth to keep them within bounds. The precaution seemed needless, though in touch with the general economic plan. Elsewhere the grass lay discouragingly dead and trodden, without a suggestion of what was to come.

After a few days the sharp edge of the air was blunted, and as the sap rose and rioted along the patient tree-trunks it set the dry bark thinking, and swelled the millions of leaf-buds till they showed misty reds and browns and pale yellows against the cold blue of the sky. One evening a warm rain fell ; the angel on the meeting-house steeple veered, and blew his long trumpet toward the south; and when the sun shone at next mid-day, the trees of the fields clapped their hands.

Now the contagion of growth had seized them every one ; and this May morning, as we strolled along in the dew after our six o'clock breakfast, spoiling our shoes and trailing our flannel gowns, we saw that the pap-poose buds had dropped great hanging sheaths, and let out soft pale-green baby leaves that were ready to shift for themselves with the rashness of youth. The maples were bright atop, the horse-chestnuts held up great bou-quets of fringed white and green. Everywhere grew yellow buttercups. Red sorrel in the fields, red colum-bine in crevices of the rocks ; the old, barren earth had indeed broken forth into singing, and these were her first quivering chords. Painted-cup was gay in the meadows, Jack-in-the-pulpit was ready for his sermon, and the swamp was one fog of leaves.

Coming suddenly upon a story-and-a-half house at a turn in the road, we stopped to admire the vines that clambered up by the brown picket fence, and hung themselves over when they could no longer climb. There were bittersweet from the woods, and wild clem-atis ; and tangled with this transplanted growth were sweet peas and nasturtiums, reaching foolish tendrils nowhere, or clinging to spears of grass that bent to every breath of wind.

"Come right along in — right along in," said Uncle Arad, planting his stout staff in our direction. "She'll be proper glad to see you."

" But at this time,"— we objected.

" Land ! what time do ye s'pose it is ? We get our breakfast 'long o' the robins ; an' they don't waste none o' the dew-time, I reckon. Why, Aunt Tishy she got her bakin' done an hour ago, an' hes jest be'n up garret for a passel o' rags. She'll be tickled enough to hev you two come in an' help her sort colors. Rag mats, y' know."

We needed no other invitation. The cool, clean kitchen, with its scoured floor and wide fireplace, where two sticks were making bright embers, was the main room of the house. Besides this, its roof covered a tiny, shut-up parlor, a bedroom on one side the chimney, and a large pantry and milkroom on the other. The window that looked toward the meeting-house was brilliant with scarlet geraniums that love the sunniness and moisture of a kitchen. A tabby cat curled on the hearth gave a homey look to the somewhat bare room. We had been frequent visitors at the house since our coming to Hilltop early in the spring, and our presence was no more disturbing to the cat than to Aunt Tishy.

Uncle Arad sat down before the fire with his hat on, and leaned both hands on his staff.

" She was a school-teacher some years back," he began; "an' what she don't know how to do " —

Uncle Arad's pride in his wife's attainments came to no conclusion.

" My other Mis' Ridge," he added, " sent the little

uns to school to her when she wa'n't more'n fifteen ;
now, was ye ? "

" Sixteen that spring Ann died," said Aunt Tishy,
cutting strips of red flannel which we begged to sew
together and roll into balls.

" Ann come nex' to the boy," said Uncle Arad meditatively. " Samwell, then Ann, then Thurzy, then Al-
miry. All of 'em went afore their ma. Seem's though
'twas some other world them days. An' now they're
gone where the streets is paved with gold, an' money
can't do 'em a mite o' good. An' here Jess hes up an
left me all his prop'ty. Curi's. It kind o' tires me to
think on 't. Can't take it with me, as they say, when
I've got to le' go my hold here. Not a soul to leave it
to 'cept the missionaries, an' 'twouldn't be a drop in
the buckit to them."

The old man got up, heavy with thought, and sat
down on the doorsill.

" 'Tis a terrible responsibility," said Aunt Tishy
softly, taking up the burden where he dropped it.
" Sometimes I think — and then again I let it alone.
But it does seem — doesn't it ? — as if when we've
got through with it we ought to fix it so as some of
our sort could have the use of it. I never believed
in missionarying so much as some. If a man has a call
to go amongst the heathen, I'm not going to put blocks
in his way. But when he expects a woman and little
children to live there with him, and bear the brunt of

it, and keeps the blessing to himself — why, it gets me
right up in arms. Let him self-sacrifice if he wants to.
I like to see a man that can. But I don't know. I've
thought and thought."

There was a long pause. The cat rose and stretched
herself, and tried her claws on her mistress's apron.

" There, Tildy, I knew you'd do it," she said mildly,
as the red and black strips slid to the floor. " See
what a mess you've made ! No, you know I can't have
you in my lap. Don't you see I had my strips all
sorted ? "

The cat listened with a bored air, turned resignedly
away, and jumped for her master's shoulder.

" That's Tildy all over ! " said Aunt Tishy, making
a deeper lap for her balls. " If I won't have her she
goes straight to him. She thinks she's had her own
way now. But about that money. I wish I could
have a sort of leading of Providence, such as some folks
have. I think and think till it seems as if I couldn't.
You wonder if there isn't some of my folks needing it,
you say. Well, yes, I'm free to tell you, plenty of
them. But there's one of his sort that I do feel a drawing towards. He's his sister's — well there, you don't
know. But he had one sister, Samiry, and she didn't
do well marrying. That is, in one way."

"Smirymus wus her name," put in Uncle Arad.
" 'Twa'n't Scriptur'. but it b'longed to some o' them
countries."

" All his folks and hers set against it," continued
Aunt Tishy, " but she would have him, and she did.
He was a wild harum-scarum sort of boy, mighty fond
of his book, though. But he was different. He was
made different, I say; and the old folks didn't know
how to get along with him any more than if he'd been
a live scarecrow. He was full of his tricks, and they
didn't have any too much patience. Folks didn't have,
very often, in those days. There was everything to do,
and not much to do with, and they couldn't put up
with fooling. Young folks had to walk straight. If a
boy had got to man's size, he must toe the mark or take
a birching. And Abner couldn't. I always would
stand up for him. I said then, and I say it now, it was
a shame to whip a boy for laughing on a Sunday. He
was a pretty boy too. There wasn't one in school I set
more store by than him — always ready to get a pail of
water recess time, and then he'd want to pass it round
in school. I couldn't say no after he'd spent all his
play-time to get it; but when he passed it round there'd
be such a jumping and squealing that I knew some mischief was afoot. He was just as sober as a judge, and I
couldn't find out for the life of me till little Billy Riggs
told on him. He said when the little boys bent down
their heads to do sums, Abner passed the dipper over,
and a trickle went right down their necks. But he
never seemed to do it, and try my best I couldn't find
out if 'twas more than an accident.

" He was kind-hearted, but the sort that can't be
happy unless they're in mischief.   He knew every weed
that ever grew round the swamp, and was always getting into difficulties with his muddy clothes and what
not.   He was always tearing his jackets too.   And I
can fairly see him now, tetering way out on an oak-
limb to get a peek into a bird's nest.   The birds didn't
care.   They thought he was another kind of one so
long as he didn't
have four legs.   He
knew   just   what
every   bird   sung,
and just how they
called to each other, and he
could make sounds like every
one of them.   Why, I've heard
a pewee answer back to him
time and again.   He never took
their eggs nor disturbed them any way ; and the old
robin that had a nest right out here in the cherry-
tree would let him come close up to her when she
was brooding, and never stir.   She'd kind of cock
her head on one side, and look him over as if she
was taking his measure and calculating what sort of a
nest he was likely to build.   Like as not he'd fall out
of the tree, forgetting where he was, with his mind
somewhere else, and 'twas bad for his clothes.   I do
suppose that boy's back smarted from one week's end

to the other, let alone the scratches he got from the
trees. But he wasn't any coward. I've seen the tears
come to his eyes when I've read stories in school —
well, I won't tell you what about. I was young then,
but I ought to have known better. There's enough to
cry about when real trouble comes. But Abner never
cried on his own account. I can say that for him.

"Well, he wanted to be somebody, he said; and
when he was old enough they put him to shoemaking
with Uncle Israel Ball. Uncle Israel pegged right
down to work, and wanted everybody to do the same.
He was clever enough; but there wasn't ever any fun
in him, and he couldn't see the use of it. You couldn't
eat it nor drink it, he said, and folks was put into this
world to make a living. 'Twas pretty hard on Abner
when he wanted learning so bad. It was meat and
drink to him. I don't know what would have become
of him if they'd let him have his head; but he'd been
some sort of a scholar, and likely as not made a living
by it."

"He run away," interpolated Uncle Arad from the
doorsill.

"Yes," sighed Aunt Tishy, "he ran away; and when
they got him back his father was considerable stricter
with him."

"He thrashed 'im," said Uncle Arad, bending his
neck to give Tabby a comfortable perch.

"Well, so they said," replied Aunt Tishy mildly,

" and I shouldn't wonder. His father wasn't a saint, and I suppose Abner was trying. But in these days they don't draw the lines so tort. Well, that boy would stay up nights to read till they took his light away; and then he'd get up soon as he could see. The minister lent him books, all about birds and beasts. He was fond of them himself. There was White's Natural History of something that he read twenty times over, till he could tell everything in it. Many a time has he sat on that doorsill and told me things I couldn't hardly believe. Seems as if he'd die if he couldn't get learning some way. I've seen some of the things he wrote out, and Parson Todd said they compared favorable with pieces he'd read in the newspapers. But as for shoemaking, 'twas of no use. The boy got so he hated the sight of a last, and a waxed end was an abomination; and his folks just about went distracted over him."

"More fools they!" piped Uncle Arad. "He wa'n't the sort that goes wrong a-purpose. They nagged an' nagged, enough to spile the soundest boy-timber that ever growed; till one day he up an' run away in good 'arnest, an' nobody to answer for't but his pa. Out West he went, like many another, an' picked up work enough; no shirk about him, an' bymeby home he come to marry our S'miry. Folks flung out everything they could about him; but Jess he stood up for Abner, and 'twas him, I reckon, helped 'em get away. Parson

Smith, over mountain, he married 'em one Monday mornin' afore breakfast. She'll tell ye the rest."

"Well," said Aunt Tishy with a comfortable sigh, "'tisn't much more to tell. He got work to do and books to study, and Samiry wrote home that he was just as good a provider as any man could be, and that she'd yet to see the day she was sorry. But 'twasn't more than two or three years before Abner took the fever and died, and she came home with her baby, and kind of faded away to nothing. The old folks did as well as they knew how for the baby, and never would give it up to his folks. Mother Ridge was a good hand with babies, easy-going and always trying to excuse their ways. We used to say she recollected when she was little. She could see good in other folks's children too, and was always laying up the reddest apples and the biggest but'nuts for them. But that poor motherless baby didn't seem to belong to Abner. He hadn't any spunk. You could put him in one place and he'd stay there. When he was big enough they tried him at shoemaking and he stuck to it. So he would to anything, though he wouldn't have thought it out for himself. When folks put things into his hands he held on. It's a born fool, they say, that hasn't got any grip.

"Well, Abner's boy made a good steady-going man, though for the life of me I couldn't feel drawn towards him, even for his poor father's sake; and when his time came, he got married and settled down. They jogged

along pretty comfortable for some years, without any
children to keep them spry and looking into things,
so that when our Abner did come along late in the day,
'twas like a miracle.

" They do say family looks and other things will
likely as not skip a generation and crop out again.
It's somehow like a piece of fallow ground. And
Abner's peculiar ways hadn't been worked up much
for one generation. First anybody knew this child
blazed right out, another Abner; the very image and
superscription of his grandpa. They couldn't have
named him better, though they didn't know it then.
He's all books, books, books, and nobody to encourage
him, only when he comes over here of a Sunday. I
have to tell him all about his grandfather, every
single word. I did hate to mention his pranks, but
there's no keeping back from this one. I've told those
same stories over and over till half the time I don't
believe them myself. He lives over there on Davy's
hill all alone, since the old gentleman died last winter.
One of the neighbors cooks his breakfast and supper,
and sees to the house, and he carries his dinner to
school, down there in the hollow. I expect he studies
too much nights, but he won't own up to it. We get
him over here to dinner Sundays; and when Uncle
Arad goes out to do the milking, I make him talk over
his plans. But, poor boy! he'll be as old as Methusaleh
before he gets money enough to go to college. You're

sure you haven't run across him anywhere? Well, I
wonder at it, for I reckon you like to climb rocks and
wade round in the swamp 'most as well as he does."

"She's comin' to the p'int now," said Uncle Arad,
slowly getting up and straightening his cramped
muscles. "I ain't in a hurry, but mebbe you two be,
an' I've seen better 'commodations than this 'ere doorsill. Tell 'em now, Aunt Tishy, what you was thinkin' about doin' for Abner. Y' see, for a spell after we
got Jess's money, we use' to lie awake nights about it.
We couldn't take it with us, an' we hated dretfully
to leave it, an' we hedn't got long to stay, though she's
nigh onto twenty year younger 'n I be. An' for one
spell last winter we'd lie an' hear the wind squealin'
round the chimbly, an' we'd say, 'Le's fix up the ol'
house, an' raise the ruff, an' make it two stories between
jints, an' put a portico over the south stoop with pil-
lers.' But, land-a-massy! what could we do with a
mansion over our heads? 'Twouldn't fit. Some cre-
turs can crawl out o' their ole shells into bigger ones
an' rattle round in 'em till they grow to fill 'em out, ef
they hev good luck. But we was too old. 'Twould
make a kind o' division amongst the neighbors too.
They wouldn't drop in after supper, friendly, if we hed
a front room all fixed up with a boughten carpet an' a
sofy. She thought we'd move the bed out, an' use the
room common. But we'd miss it in case of sickness.
Top chamber rooms don't fit old folks with stiff j'ints.

You want to go right from the kitchen fire to bed. An'
a front room ain't reel comfortable anyway y' can fix it.
You set round kind o' starchy like comp'ny, an' nothin'
to say. Folks ain't plagued with idees when they live
in the front room. Now she'll go on."

Thus encouraged, Aunt Tishy took up the dropped
thread of her story again, while the cat crept out behind the rose bushes to lay plans for a robin that stalked
just beyond reach.

" What I was coming to was about Abner. We'd be
glad enough to help him if only we knew how. But
that's the business that keeps us awake nights. He's
in favor of giving the boy enough right out to take him
square through college ; but I can't seem to see my
way clear to it. Of course he's our folks, but then —
and I get to thinking it over and over till it don't seem
to have any sense. I shouldn't want folks to give me
money that they could use for themselves, and he's
enough like his grandpa to say he wouldn't touch it.
You can't give money to folks same as if 'twas garden
sauce, or maybe a piece of sperrib at butchering time
that was more than you knew what to do with yourself. I'm free to tell you it's harder for me not to hold
on to money than 'tis for him. It's partly in the blood,
and it's partly bringing up. He was forehanded for
those days when I married him; and I'd been earning
my money at the hardest in a district school, and board-
ing round. There wasn't anybody to look out for me.

But there, I shall think it all out some night when I'm lying awake, and then I'll know for sure. If young folks had to lie awake the way old folks do, they wouldn't make so many mistakes bringing up their families. It's so kind of peaceful along before cock-crow, and the earth seems so small flying 'round there amongst the stars, that your own affairs don't loom up to the daytime size, and you can get a sight at them all round."

The tall clock in the corner ticked in an important way, and flashed back at the sun that had just looked into its face. Tabby slipped in, licking her chops with a foretaste of spring robin, and lay down discontented at the feet of her mistress, who added : —

"Providence didn't see fit, all these years, to send us anybody to provide for specially : — Why, Arad Ridge ! " she cried, with such energy that Tabby bristled and sprang for the door ; "why, for goodness' sake, don't we two adopt *him!* Maybe that's what Providence meant all this time ! "

As we went out under the cherry-trees two robins stood at gaze in a straight line and watched us severely. In the tall Norway spruce by the back gate there was a sound like touching a dry leaf followed by the *quip* of hurrying wings. Something suspected us. Two wrens were building in a box on a pole, singing as they built. It sounded like " blowing a pipe under water." Orioles flashed by with their flying *thir-r-r, thir-r-r ;* a song sparrow was trying variations on his *quis-ka-dee* theme. The air was full of the divine scent of apple blossoms, some trees still in pink bud, fresh and sweet as if this were their first experiment in a waiting world.

A young man passed us beside the garden wall, and lifted his hat. It was the first attention of the kind that Hilltop had granted us, and we promptly made up our minds that this could be no other than Abner the Second. It was Saturday and a holiday. The stranger carried a mighty bouquet of wild columbine. As we went on the gate creaked behind us, and we fell to wondering if Aunt Tishy would recognize in this unusual visit a leading of Providence.

III

A LITTLE WORLD

IF clouds could pick up individual houses as one gathers flowers or berries, and drop them again recklessly, Hilltop might have been the result of a cloudburst at an inauspicious moment. Perched on the tip of a rocky plateau, stood the orthodox meeting-house,

to which all but a favored half-dozen families had to climb for their weekly sermon. Around the edifice, as the slow imagination of the elders named it, spread a discouraged common, less than a half-acre in extent, zigzagged by footpaths, and foiled in its tardy attempts at greenness by sheep that roamed and nibbled at will, and made quiet pictures, restful to the eye. One could hear the sound of their grazing across the common on still days when the world lay asleep. A small box of a brown church called 'Piscopal, with a cross on its steeple, stood blinking over the way, with shutterless windows. The weather-beaten door, that had not been unlocked since the society died out, groaned dismally in a high wind; and children ran away from it. A haunted church is far more ghostly than a haunted house, for its possibilities are as ten to one.

On a sunny slope still higher than the common, 'Squire 'Lias's house stood, cheerful and inviting, catching the light of the sun before he dropped to unseen depths behind the opposite hill, and flashing it back from two rows of shining windows, two oval cross-eyes above the front door, and the one small, arched garret window over all.

Mrs. 'Lias, the presiding genius of the place through the day, was the serene mother of sons and daughters who came home with large families to Thanksgiving, but left the great house lonely through the long summer days, so that it was easy to secure a comfortable shelter during the weeks of heat that depopulate cities. We were the only summer boarders that had, as yet, toiled up the steeps to Hilltop, and the chances were that its casino-days were as far removed as the millennium. Once a week the stage climbed slowly up and up and up; the driver halted by the town pump, took a

package from his breast pocket and handed it to the
storekeeper, Captain Saul, who blew the dust out of a
cigar-box before transferring the precious foreign intel-
ligence to its keeping. The postmaster had been a
seafaring man in his youth long past, and now kept
house in a small room back of the store. There he
took his letters, and the two or three weekly papers
subscribed for by the moneyed men of the place, who
would call for them in
the evening. Seated be-
side his one window,
with a thrifty lilac bush
tapping on the pane, he
took what he called
solid comfort in looking
over the mail, reading
the addresses and post-
marks on the letters,

and guessing who wrote each one and for what purpose it was written, before he laid them carefully by
in the cigar-box to be called for, or forwarded to
remote farms by some so-called neighbor. It beguiled
the lingering hours, and furnished abundant food
for thought and conjecture. His teakettle always
sang fitfully on a stove not much too large for it,
unless its room were needed for a skillet of beans
or plum duff. We often made small errands to
the store, hoping to coax a sea-yarn out of Captain

Saul. It was well that the errands were of minor importance.

" Well, no, miss, I ain't got number eighty, that's a fact; but here's a spool of twenty left if that'll do you. I bought that thread back in the seventies."

The Captain assured us that he never extortioned anybody, but that he couldn't afford noway to have clearin' out sales as they did over mountain. Apparently he had never had " a home and folks " anywhere. He had sailed to heathenish lands, he told us, but was always in a hurry to get home again and stow away his toggery ship-shape above high-water mark.

His tales of the sea were not imaginative. He could tell the plain truth with the accuracy of the table in addition, but could no more spin a yarn than weave a web. If he had been born a spider, the flies would have had no occasion to complain of him. The element of romance was wholly lacking in his simple life. " I've heer'd the sea roar and the wind howl," he would say meditatively, with one elbow on the counter; " but bein' ashore's another thing — another thing." When asked to explain, he had no answer ready; and while solemnly thinking it over, a customer would occasionally surprise him, and so entirely turn the tide of his thoughts that we never knew precisely how the difference between the sea and land struck him.

At one time all Hilltop thought that Aunt Minerva Pease, a widow of long standing, looked with favor on

Captain Saul; but as the look was not returned, nothing came of it, and the subject, after much handling, was reluctantly dropped. Yet Aunt Minerva, who lived in a house of her own, had five hundred dollars laid up in the bank, as every one knew, and was not a bad-looking woman for one of her age. The Captain was plainly lacking in foresight, if his other faculties were tolerably well preserved. The conjecture caused a lively ripple in the community, that kept it in a state of sparkle for weeks.

'Squire 'Lias's comfortable house commanded a view of the hill that led to the town; but away on the west was another summit that we had not explored. Early one bright afternoon we started to look down, if possible, into the mysterious region where the sun disappeared every night. Our hostess was concerned lest we should be all tuckered out, and late to supper besides, and suggested our taking the horse and shay. But as any horse, however recommended, was to us an unknown quantity, we preferred the ills we were accustomed to, and set off sturdily on foot. Passing the common, with its white flock that nibbled all day and gave no thought to digestion, we stopped a moment at Uncle Arad's gate, that hospitably swung in. The vines were reaching out in a clamorous, wild way, and the air was bitter-sweet with cherry blossoms. A second turning to the west led to higher ground, where we stopped to watch Hurry Brook, as it held the little

burying ground gently in its left elbow, and, after a
caressing pause, dashed on under the low bridge that
helped the road climb the hill.

At the foot of the ascent
stood the brown schoolhouse.
in the very heart of temptation,
where Abner the Second ruled
over the entire coming generation of Hilltop. We could hear
the shrill voices spelling dreadful words of four syllables as
we climbed the hill. Two grin-
ning heads like live gargoyles
bent out at two windows to
beam upon us, and the spelling
voices fell a little, then rose
again in a higher key. like those
of interrupted katydids. The brook
beckoned and the birds enticed, holding the little schoolhouse in the spell
of their enchantment; and the young
of all but man made glorious holiday.

Long Hill stretched on alluringly,
with thick woodland on one side and lonely
dwellings on the other, set close to the highway for what scant company they might find in the
few passers-by. It was simply a wood-road that led
nowhere. If we had been a circus procession with

a brass band, we could not have called more heads to the windows. Now and then an overgrown girl came boldly out to shoo a foolish hen that flew with needless squawking into a new flower-bed, and was left to over-turn the work of days, while we passed in review, con-scious that the fashion of our gowns and the faults of our hats would be repeated for years.

Here we rested to look down on the little world below. We could track civilization by the rows of cherry-trees, like great white bouquets, marking every homestead. The peach-trees added a pink tinge to the green and white world, and a faint odor of opening apple-buds mingled with the tonic of the cherry. Toward the south, Hurry Brook fell into Roaring River, and, just where they joined forces, the sawmill under its rickety shed was making a huge log into slabs. The sound was not discordant at this distance. Nature manages her chords with discretion, even utilizing man's discords. A single tree-trunk, hewn level on the upper side, bridged the brook perilously a few feet before the stream fell into the rocky bed of the river, and hung full ten feet above the foaming water. Here the saw-miller's wife, whose head grew suddenly dizzy, once made herself famous by jumping into the stream from the middle of the uncertain bridge, and wading out unharmed. In the dearth of talk the story grew as large. if not as fast, as those of town origin, and prom-ised a grandmotherly heroine to future generations.

In that event we, too, might win local fame. So with sketch-books already half filled, we drew the log bridge, the sawmill, and the two mad streams that suddenly lost their united selves in a gorge between the hills.

Hours slid away like moments; the twilight was long in coming; and as we went on, the ridge of the world seemed to stretch from east to west before us. The trees were wrenched and twisted, mercilessly deformed and bowed by years of northern blasts. There was an abrupt descent in the path of the sun that daily hid itself from Hilltop long in advance of almanac time. It was too late for us to follow; so we turned aside, and in the deeps of the wood, a little lower down, sat on a fallen tree-trunk to rest.

Suddenly, as from some strange planet, if not from the sun itself, whose rays made dancing green and orange tints before our eyes, two figures appeared on the brow of the hill. We sat in the shadow of a great oak-trunk and waited, but they did not pass. Their voices came to us clearly, as they turned with the full light on their young faces, and looked out over the wonderful scene. The young girl was bareheaded, and her hat, swung by its strings, was full of red columbine.

"No, Abner," she was saying, as we tried, guiltily, not to hear, "it's of no use. I shall not change my mind. You are going to be somebody in the world, and

I think too much of you to be a drag. Besides, I am older than you. You will understand it for yourself as soon as you go away from here. Think of a freshman at Yale — engaged! "

She laughed, a hearty, ringing laugh ; but the young man stood, motionless and unresponsive, with bowed head.

" College life will make a new world for you, Abner, and nobody can be gladder than I. You will write me about it, I know."

" No," said Abner the Second, raising his head, " I shall not write."

" Then I shall be grieved and disappointed," said the other. " You won't keep all your good times to yourself. That isn't like you, Abner."

There was a pause, and we dared not breathe.

" No, I don't care for anybody else," she continued, " but I know for certain that my judgment in this is better than yours. I'm older, you know! "

And so, with strong emphasis on the word that set

her to judge her young lover, she turned, and the two passed out of sight.

Next morning we strolled over to the house beyond the common and found it unoccupied. The kitchen door stood wide open, and the sleepy cat lay in a streak of sunshine, making up for a prowling night. The kettle sang on the longest hook suspended from the crane, and puffed out spiteful jets of steam for its own amusement. We waited awhile, with our tribute of columbine, wild flowers, and saxifrage, until the sound of voices in the garden guided us down the walk between the cherry-trees, whose falling petals made a summer snow flurry.

"Only jest look at 'er, puttin' her posy-seeds into the ground," said Uncle Arad. "You'd think she's goin' to plant an acre lot."

We had no other greeting. Uncle Arad sat contentedly on the garden bench, watching Aunt Tishy as she dug shallow trenches and dropped seeds with generous, loving care. The accustomed tall silk hat of another generation was replaced by a rakish straw with narrow brim that might have been great-grandson to the other, though not in lineal descent.

"I'm doing just as near like Nature as I can," replied Aunt Tishy, from the deeps of a green gingham sunbonnet. "There isn't a stingy thread about her anywhere as I can see, and I calculate I've looked close year after year. Just see how she gives the seeds wings, and sticks them onto the sheep's backs, and trusts the birds with 'em, and sows 'em broadcast from the trees to be trod on and ground up by wheels and lost. If a quarter of mine come up they'll do well."

"Now, don't y' giv' in to Natur'; jest expect 'em all to come up," said Uncle Arad, thrusting his stick into the soft mould and making mathematical patterns. "She'll git the better of y' every time ef y' do. Many's the Sunday forenoon I've stood fust on one foot and then on t'other, a-watchin' that cre'tur' on the meetin'-us steeple a-p'intin' nor'east; an' ef ever I stayed to home to save my clo'es, no sooner 'd the second bell stopped ringin', too late to start, than round she'd flop an' p'int due west, goin' round by the nor-rard, too, like's not, which ain't a sign o' good weather."

"Uncle Arad, that's an angel," said Aunt Tishy, with as much emphasis as was compatible with her temporary obscurity.

"Angel or woman, I d' know," said Uncle Arad addressing us collectively; "but she's plaguey contrairy all the same. Don't y' recollect the time we went over mountain to Isr'el Beerses buryin'? I got ol' Poll hitched up, sun shinin' an' birds pipin' away, an' it begun to thunder. But I jest tucked in an extry buffalo under the wagon seat, an' a big umberill, an' says I to Aunt Tishy, 'Put on y'r ole things outside. Ef it's got to rain, 'twill.' I declar' for 't ef them black clouds didn't jest pile right up in the teeth o' the

wind. The trees sagged, an' the' was a roar follerin' as
ef the end o' the world 'd come. But I wa'n't goin' to
back out an' lose thet fun'ral. We hedn't be'n over
mount'in fer more'n a year; an' Isr'el was a sort o'
distant relation. His father's brother married my
mother's half-sister for his second wife, an' one o' the
boys was named Arad for me."

"And it didn't rain a drop," said Aunt Tishy, standing bent a moment with both hands on her knees, then
straightening to shake out her apron. "If you don't
want to get dirt in your finger-nails, just dip them in
flour to begin with."

"No more it didn't," said Uncle Arad, ignoring the
aside. "Them clouds jest rolled round the mount'in
an' let drop some'ers off to west'ard. That extry buffalo did the bus'ness. You jest go right along when y'
git ready, pay no sort o' 'tention to the weather, an' ten
to one 'twill hold up for ye. But you stan' on one foot
a spell, teterin' in yer mind whether you'll hev yer
own way er git wet, an' you'll ketch it for sure. Go
right along about yer bus'ness an' the weather'll most
giner'ly stan' out o' yer way. It's so about sights o'
things, only I didn't find it out soon enough. A young
feller'll hang round a likely girl a spell, an' mebbe let
somebody get ahead of him, when ef he'd jest walked
right up to 'er fair an' square, he'd got her, easy's
preachin'."

" Don't you be too sure of that," warned Aunt Tishy.

" You didn't get me first time asking by any manner of means."

" Nor the second neither," chuckled Uncle Arad, with a great sense of humor; " but I got ye. That's the p'int."

" Last night," said Aunt Tishy with dignity, as she loosened the warm strings of her sunbonnet, " I saw our Abner walking up toward Peter's Hill with that Brumley girl."

" Yes, yes," said Uncle Arad shrewdly, "jest like 'er. She set her cap for 'im 'long about the time we 'dopted him. Anybody could see that with half an eye."

" But she won't catch him," said Aunt Tishy with spirit. " She's all of three years the oldest, if she does keep it close. He'll find it out sometime. You can't cheat a man forever. She's well enough, but Abner'll be apt to look higher. I don't believe she's going to get around him."

"Say nothin', say nothin'," put in Uncle Arad. " Jest let 'im git off to college. He'll find girls there thicker'n huckleberries. But ef you go to sayin' a word, 'twill spile it all."

And not one word could we whisper to exonerate the Brumley girl. We were simply eavesdroppers, and must hide our guilty secret. But we did enjoy saying to ourselves on the way home that the world's judgments were cruelly wrong, and that it was a worth-while kind of girl who would try to make a man promise to write her about his every-day affairs, and so tide over the time till he could see things clearly himself, instead of cutting off his future right there in the solemn light of the dying sun, and making the whole thing tragic. `

IV

CAP'N SAUL

THE rain came all aslant, and at times quite obscured the angel on the steeple, that had flown frantically at all points of the compass since daybreak. The fruit-trees were bedraggled, and a snow of cherry blossoms had left the trees bare of beauty. The battle of the wind and shriek of the storm reminded one of the sea,

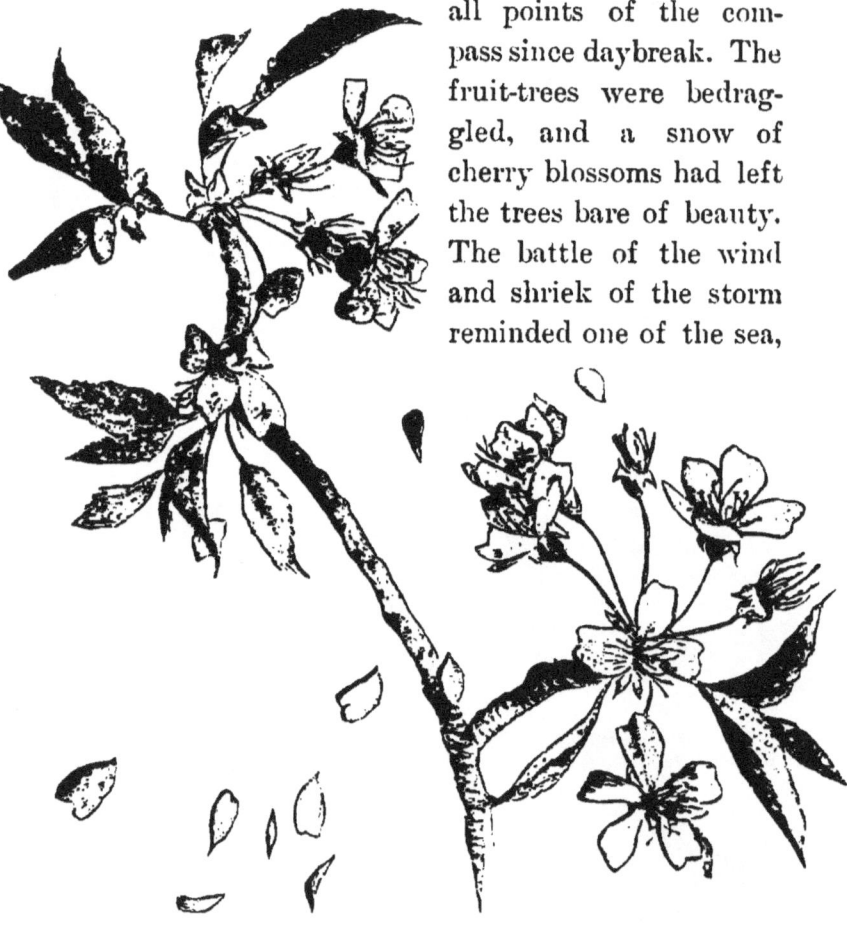

and suggested Captain Saul. On such a day, with no human possibility of a stray customer, might we not reasonably expect from him the yarn that our wiliest devices had thus far failed to suggest?

So we sallied out, with umbrellas steering us against our will, and mackintoshes that flapped wildly and flattened us against the fence as we struggled to open the gate. There was a brief lull as we crossed the common, reminding us of Uncle Arad's wise saw, "Never give in to the weather." But at Captain Saul's three steep steps the angel veered again, and we were driven quite into the little shop before the sudden rear-charge of the gale. As the latch gave way, the Captain came leisurely forward, pulling down his sleeves, and to our joy asked us into the back room to dry off. Thus far were the fates uncommonly propitious. While the postmaster set our streaming umbrellas in a tub, and hung our mackintoshes on the backs of his only chairs, to drip on the hearth, we ventured feebly to ask for a paper of number nine needles and a ball of twine.

Captain Saul said he knew we must want them two things bad, and he'd do his best to hunt 'em up for us. There was an unexpected twinkle in his eyes; and when he came back, package in hand, after opening creaky drawers that hitched at the corners, we owned up and begged for a story.

It seemed to strike a deep-lying vein of humor of whose very existence we had been doubtful. We were,

in a way, at the Captain's mercy, and could see a
slowly forming wrinkle of laughter on his leathery
cheeks, as he moved around clearing decks and making
things taut. His housekeeping seemed accidental, and
dependent on circumstances. We had hit upon a day
when things were not redded up.

Above the small pine table by the window that over-
looked the garden patch hung a great cage; and an
evil-eyed parrot, with shining feathers and cruel beak,
clawed up and down its wires, and laughed at us, but
not covertly. It was an embarrassing situation; and
the Captain, with rare tact, drew the green cambric
cover over the cage and said soothingly, "There, there,
Quilp, good-night, now, and stop your nonsense." A
gurgled good-night came lazily from behind the screen,
and we were secure from an interruption that had
threatened to ruin our plans.

"You wanted them things so bad now," continued
the Captain, with fresh access of humor, "that I don't
know but what I had ough' to tell you a yarn to pay
you for the trouble of comin' after 'em such a day. So
I'll just hang your things up on a hook and let 'em
drean, and wipe off a couple of chairs for you. You
see I don't have comp'ny every day, let alone cus-
tomers."

The Captain reached to a high line over the stove
for his dish-towel, and scrubbed the chairs with hospitable intent; then drew an old-style linen duster over

his blue flannel short sleeves for manners, and sat down on a cracker box at the end of the table, where a jack-knife, and block of wood partly whittled into boat shape, lay at hand.

The lilac outside bowed and scraped against the small window, and dragged its heavy blossoms to and fro, as if trying to get in; and a homely old heirloom of a clock, whose case touched the low ceiling, swung its pendulum in a mournful way, and dismally marked the time. A

 mariner's compass hung beside it, and seashells, great and small, perched on every ledge that offered a foothold. A hammock, close reefed, depended double from a hook, and dingy fishing-tackle of salty flavor huddled in a corner behind it.

With the rash confidence of youth we broke silence by saying that it must be lonesome living all by one's self.

"I s'pose," said the Captain cheerfully, "you've got Mis' Pease on your mind. Most folks has. Time enough for me when they've all had their say out. Fact is, there ain't much to talk about here. But I don't look like a man to be drove, now, do I? An old sea cap'n's pretty well seasoned, and he can get his bearin's most as good as a 'longshoreman, now, can't he?"

We dared not deny it.

The parrot rustled in its darkened cage, and suddenly shrieked " Good-morning ! " with an effect quite disproportioned to the cause. It had dragged the cover down till the ring hole came on a level with its beak, and one wicked eye looked at us askance. The Captain rose laboriously and pulled off the cover. " Got ahead of me, just as you allays do, you ! If these ladies don't mind, let out your talk now, but don't you dare to swear ! Mind !" The parrot, with human contrariness, kept still with a show of not hearing a word that had been said.

" The generality of folks," said the Captain, drawing his knife-blade firmly across the sole of his shoe, " manages to get some sort of a play spell into their threescore and ten, even when their nighest don't suspicion it. When a man's stiddy and solemn in his ways, they reckon there ain't any fun in him. But I ain't sure but what it's goin' on inside of the best of 'em. Some things ain't made to show on top. I reckon the mains'l gets jest as much good of the breeze as the top-gallants does, if it don't make words about it. You see the folks in this 'ere town don't know as much as they think they do about me, and I'd just as lieves they wouldn't."

It was a delicate way of confiding in us, which we appreciated.

" Some folks, now, can reel off yarns, fathoms of 'em, long as they can hold out at the windlass. But nothin' ever come to me but once, and that I've kept close, many's the year. Somehow in the middle of the night, or on a blowy day like this 'ere, I get to thinkin', thinkin' — and mebbe it's good to get it off'n my mind. Mebbe it's better not to be buried with me, as if 'twas a wrong to somebody another, which it wa'n't."

The Captain closed one eye, and sighted his boat from stem to stern.

" When I wa'n't much more'n a lad," he continued cautiously, " I was off to one of them heathenish countries that you've studied about in your school-books, and we went ashore of a Sunday. My old mother over mountain brought me up to go to meetin'; so I looked round for a steeple, and calculated I'd save up my money whilst the other boys spreed it. Pretty soon I fetched up to a queer place with a cross on top. You don't mind my tellin' you there was as pretty a girl as ever you see, a dippin' her little fingers into a dish right by the door. I didn't know it was holy water then. But she crossed herself and went in, and I follered, expectin' to take a seat and hear a sermon. Down she went on her knees, and I standin' there like an ijit.

" You see, I wa'n't used to sayin' my prayers afore folks. Why, I'd as soon a kissed my old mother outside here on the green. So I stood 'round a spell and watched when she went out, and follered her. I'd made up my mind she wa'n't no heathen, or she wouldn't say her prayers. She wa'n't exactly white, and she wa'n't a colored person, by no manner of means. She was just that soft kind of nice dark white, with eyes black as huckleberries, and white teeth, and a great rope of black hair braided down her back, big as a ship's cable. You mayn't be sure she was good lookin', but I give you my word for't. Well, my mind was made up in a minit, and gener'ly I ain't a quick man. Only I wondered what my poor old mother 'd say. But I could tell her the girl was pious, sure.

"That night I went to the priest, and found out her name and all I could about her. 'Twa'n't easy. She didn't have any folks, only her old grandmother, and they had got just a little money, enough to keep 'em along in a poor way. I told the priest I'd be obligated to him if he'd sort o' keep an eye on her till I come 'round next time, and he said he would. I didn't know whether to believe him or not; but he was a clever sort of fellow, if he was a priest; and if he didn't quite understand, we made signs and sort o' guessed. And he could talk our talk a little. We was takin' on a load of — well, there, no matter. You'd know where it was, mebbe, and it's jest as well not. But we stayed a week; and every blessed day that Marree, they called her, went to church, sun-up. I was on hand, I tell you! And one day I walked along with her, and she seemed to know what I was tryin' to say. I'd had my grog along with the boys till then, but I tell you I never touched it again when I went ashore. We had to have it reg'lar for rations on the Mary Jane, you know. That's our ship.

" You mayn't be willin' to believe it, but next year
when we touched at them — when we got there again,
straight to the church went I, and there, true's you're
alive, was Marree, a kneelin' down right in the middle
aisle. When she'd said her prayers, I stood stock still,
and she looked at me, and then the color went all the
way up to her eyes. I hope she wouldn't mind my
tellin' you. And we found the priest, and he married
us. Don't sound true, now, does it? But so it was.
And I'm a married man to this day. And she took me
to her house, and told her grandma, and the poor old
lady was blind, and couldn't see ; so Marree made me
kneel down for her to put her two wrinkled old hands
on my head. She jabbered something too, but I
couldn't understand ; and she couldn't hear a word
I said, though Marree could talk to her.

" Three years I went back and forth, the sea ragin'
and the wind howlin' and the sun beatin' down ; and
the last time Marree cried to go home with me. She'd
got so we could talk a little mixed talk then. She
could say some of my words, and she'd laugh till she
cried hearin' me try her lingo. You see, I hadn't got
to be cap'n yet, and I couldn't take her with me. But
she promised to write, and just as soon as I got my
ship I said she should come home with me. I hadn't
ever broke it to my old mother, and she died afore 1
could make up my mind to tell her. It lay heavy on
me for years. It does now. I'd ought to have told

her, poor old woman! but I knew she'd make a fuss,
because her plans was all staked out for a girl over
mountain that she knew for certain would make me a
good wife. Then 'twas two years that we didn't go
there, and I got just four letters. You see 'twas hard
spellin' out our words."

The captain choked a little and coughed to hide it,
and Quilp laughed fiendishly, biting the wires and
clawing up and down the cage.

" But what little I did get I kept in mother's Bible.
It was like a little bit of the Good Book to me, and it's
stayed there ever since. I didn't look the way I do
now," he added apologetically, with a brave effort at
cheerfulness.

" By no manner of means. When Tom Stow was
home — him that shipped first with me — 'twas last
year he come — says he, 'Saul Lamb, you ain't changed
a mite since first we sailed seas together.' But, Lordy!
I come home, and I looked into that little glass over
yonder where I do my Sunday shavin', and says I right
out loud, 'Saul Lamb, did you always look so?'"

There was a long pause.

" And did she come home with you?" we ventured to
ask.

The captain shook his head and brushed the back of
his hand across one eye. It was the hand that held the
jack-knife.

" When I went back the priest was dead, and the old

lady was dead; seemed as if everybody was gone.
Some young folks tried to make me think she was
underground. But I didn't believe it. And one of
'em brought out a little mite of a baby and put it into
my arms and shut its eyes, and made signs that Marree
had one like it, and now both of 'em was gone. But I
wouldn't believe it. I darsent. So 'round I went,
tryin' and tryin' to find out. 'Twas the same old story.
You see, I hadn't heard a word from Marree the latter
part of the time. It was pretty soon after sailin' that I
got her letters. Mostly folks didn't seem to know what
I wanted. It just about killed me to think I might 'a'
known and couldn't, because they couldn't talk. They
wouldn't understand, though I spoke up loud and slow,
as if I was sayin' a hard spellin' lesson. But nobody
could say a thing satisfactory. The more they tried,
the worse off I was.

" Year by year I went back, and every time I hunted
and I s'arched. The last time an old woman got hold
of me, and she took me backside the church and showed
me a place with two boards, a little and a big one, and
some writing that the rain had washed out long ago, so
there wa'n't three words left. And I don't doubt now
but what she must be a lyin' there. I don't want to
see salt water, nor a ship, nor a sailor again, as long as I
live. She must be gone, for she set great store by me.
though you mightn't think it. If I'd been commodore
she couldn't have made more of me. I didn't look the

way I do now. I was a lad once, but 'twas years ago."

There was a long, solemn pause.

"When my posy beans blow," the captain continued, "and the trees all round get white and bloomy, and I hear the sheep a nibblin', and the birds makin' their nests and singin' about it all, says I to myself, 'I don't know as I want any better heaven, fur's I'm concerned.' I ain't much of a religious man, but I'm gettin' old; and when the wind blows, and the snow piles up and cuts me off till I'm all alone, and fearful lonesome, I get a sort of hankerin' after the Better Country the parson tells about. And it does seem to me, if she's there, she won't be a mite more contented than she used to be, even with the little one to tend, till I get there too. We can say all we want to there, don't you think? and understand all that's said, I reckon, and—I don't suppose I'll look the way I do now."

We had blown half-way to the town pump when we heard him calling, "Say you!" and turned back. He made a speaking trumpet of his hands, but we had to go quite back to the steps and listen, as he bent down humbly to say:

"You'll recollect, won't you, that was all a joke about Mis' Pease?"

V

THE WIDOW PEASE

AFTER Captain Saul's story we lost all but the ordinary country interest in Mrs. Minerva Pease, and were

even mildly annoyed when our provident hostess suggested that Hilltop would better be looking out for a new storekeeper.

It was perfectly understood in church circles that Mrs. Pease had money laid up in the bank far beyond her need, and that she only required a good, smart man to manage her farm and be taken care of in return, which was clearly an economic measure when wages were high. No other motive carried weight in this rural community, where young, and consequently foolish, people were supposed to marry in haste only to repent in the scant leisure following matrimony and farm life. Marriage was an

affair of suitability, the adapting of means to an end,
and worldly advancement. "Bettering one's self," they
called it; an opinion wholly confined to remote country
places.

Mrs. Pease was a "professor" whom we had seen at
church, in false front of blue-black hair and gold-bowed
spectacles; wearing also a sombre, if not severe, expression, as befitting her widow weeds. Her pew was on a
level with the parson's own, just across the aisle, but
fully as select and uncomfortable as his, where one had
to throw the head back with the aching effect of a top
check to get a fair view of the pulpit. The aristocratic
front pew-holders were impaled, as it were, on the very
horns of the altar, but with a certain sense of distinction
that helped offset all physical inconvenience.

We came by chance upon Mrs. Minerva's house, and,
impelled by a somewhat vulgar curiosity fostered in the
stimulating atmosphere of Hilltop, made up an errand,
encouraged by our success at Captain Saul's, and
planned to stop at the door and ask our way over the
mountain. The heat of the day was so great that we
were more than once tempted to turn back before we
had trailed down through the dust and rolling stones,
and again up through dust and rolling stones and
thankee-ma'ams, to our surprised glimpse of the house
we had seen from our own windows.

One never knew to what lengths Hilltop roads might
go. After scrambling up breezy hills and cork-screw-

ing down, down into still valleys, where some small
mountain stream gleamed in the sun "like a shining
blade unsheathed," and made the meadows knee-deep
with tender grass, the road that set out so bravely

might fade grad-
ually into a cart-
path that led to
some great barn-
door, or a wood-
road that lost it-
self among the
oaks and chest-
nuts destined for
the axe.

We came at
last to the cool
lane leading
through trim
rows of great,
white - blossomed
locust - trees, to
the side porch of
a broad-fronted house that sat down like a watch-
dog, half at rest, but wholly alert to protect the
premises. This architectural peculiarity of truly old
houses has never been traced to its source with any degree of satisfaction. Uncle Arad explained to us once
that a roof of that build shed rain like a duck's back,

and could be come at from behind without a ladder, when it leaked. Before the ending of the lane, we caught a glimpse of its owner at her ironing-table, for it was yet early on a Tuesday morning.

The Sabbath-day false front had disappeared, and with it the company expression of the wearer. Her own pretty, crinkly gray hair was drawn back under a rusty black-lace cap with flat bows; but the heat of the day, combined with the dampness of violent exercise, had cajoled a few stray hairs into little dandelion curls that ringed about the withered face caressingly, as if youth had only turned the corner and might be coaxed back.

We knocked timidly at the Dutch door cleft horizontally, that stood with halves hospitably wide, leading out to a trim garden, sweet with old-fashioned "laylocks" and "pineys." The ironing-table stood directly before the entrance, taking advantage of the southerly breeze that quietly wafted in the warm odors of all outdoors.

"Over mountain?" Mrs. Pease repeated incredulously after us. "Over mountain such a day as this? Wouldn't Square 'Lias give you a lift in his buggy if he knew you'd got to go?"

It was useless to say that the buggy had no charms for us. Appearances were plainly not in our favor. We tried to make it sound probable that we were simply exploring the country for pleasure, and preferred to walk.

"You wouldn't if you'd been ironing all the morning," said Mrs. Minerva, with practical country sense. "I s'pose you don't have a mortal thing to do. I'm proper glad to set down when night comes, and let the country take care of itself. A lone woman finds steps ready provided, and don't have to go out huntin' 'em up. But do come in, if you can get by this table, or take seats out there under the grape-vine and cool off. There's quite a pretty breeze outside. You can go over mountain any day if you're so minded ; and some of 'em are bound to be cooler than this. Tuesdays gen'-rally is hot days. But I can stand that better than wet Mondays, that put your work all aback."

We waived the limited invitation to enter, and sat down contentedly under the arbor that held two seats beside the stone steps, and extended its shade as far as the latticed well. A thrifty grape-vine with no dead twigs overran the whole, and managed its thoughtless tendrils in a tidy way. Everything about the premises spoke of thriftiness and aversion to loose ends.

We suggested, as once before with good effect at Captain Saul's, that it must be lonely at night so far from neighbors, when one had no family.

"You're right there," said Mrs. Minerva, folding a pillow-case critically, and listening to the heat of an iron that she had just taken up from the stove behind her. "I never could see why a clock ticks so much louder nights. Half the time I don't hear it till Eben

Smith goes home after milkin', and then I declare if it
don't act as though 'twas alive ! I've known it to stop
a spell and hark, and then go on again.

" Do I stay here all alone ? Why, bless your hearts.
yes. Eben lives just beyond the woods there, where I
can call him with a horn any time, day or night. He
takes his meals at home, and glad enough I am to miss
the sound of his boots for a spell. But it's a relief to
his wife, I know, to have him away the heft of the
time. He's as open-mouthed as a tarrier, and many's
the time I've wished his talk would run to bark.
But I should be bad off for news if 'twa'n't for him. I
don't s'pose anybody ever dropped an idle word at the
store that he didn't pick it up and bring it home.
Likely's not he forgot his errand into the bargain, and
I had to do without codfish over Sunday."

Our hostess mused a space, and hung two pillow-cases
on a line above the stove without losing the thread of
discourse. We could easily connect what followed
with Eben's reprehensible tongue.

"Folks 'round here that don't have their own business to 'tend to have hard times getting up a match for
me every now and then. It worries them dreadfully to
think I'm lonesome. They do say Captain Saul Lamb's
lookin' out for to better himself," she added. " But
land o' Goshen ! I'd as soon sell off stock and buy a
man. Why that sof'ly kind couldn't get a cow home
by milkin'-time. And you can see for yourself he don't

keep things put up.   You can order a man 'round that
comes to you for his pay every Saturday night, and get
a good deal out of him if you keep at it; but as for
havin' one steady in the house, day in and day out, to
cook for, and wash and iron for — starched shirt bosoms
and collars — land! what fools some women be.   When
I don't feel like settin' table I just go into the butt'ry
and draw a chair up to the window lookin' out on the
meadow, and pick a cold chicken-bone, mebbe, or dish
out some baked beans to eat with my cold coffee, and
then wash my cup and spoon and saucer.   That's all
there is to it.   But think of a man's takin' vittles that
way!   I'd as li'ves have a cow in my butt'ry.

"No, I didn't do that way when I was young.   Mr.
Pease was a good provider; and we had things as comfortable as the best, and thanked Providence for it.
His folks left him some money about the time we
begun to housekeep.   We had one little girl too.
Irene, we called her, after his mother.   Year after year
we laid up money for her and allowed she'd marry well,
and have the farm after us, and a houseful of young
ones, like as not.   It hadn't ever dawned on us that
she would go first and leave us all alone.   It was like
wipin' out a long sum on a slate.   We knew, of course,
that one of us would be obliged to go first, sooner or
later, and we used to talk it over how the one that was
left would live with Irene.   I used to tell him just
where to keep his clothes and not make trouble the

way some old folks will, leavin' things at loose ends.
I didn't want him to be a burden on Irene.

"I can see her now, standin' on her little cricket that
he made for her when she was four years old; standin'
back there by the sink wipin' dishes for me. Her hair
was real pretty, and I braided it in two little round
braids that never got fuzzy. Why, she was just like a
little woman, though it wouldn't have been proper to
tell her so. She pieced a whole bed-quilt before she
five was years old; little bits of squares.

"You see, she didn't go to school, and I didn't let
her have children here to play with, so she had plenty
of time. She was better off alone. She had her rag
babies and a white kitten; and I never left her home
when I went to meetin' or sewin' society, or a funeral,
or for a walk in the buryin'-ground Sundays after tea.
Why, she knew more than four hundred Bible verses,
if you'll believe it, before her bed-quilt was done.
Four hundred and twenty-seven it was. She used to
say, 'Suffer the little children to come and see me, and
forbid them not.' And it affected her pa. He wouldn't
let me change it, and so she always said it that way.
But he didn't have the care of her bringing up. He
was for lettin' her go to school with all the rag-tag from
down the hill."

Mrs. Minerva took up the tip of her apron and passed
it across one eye, while with the other she watched the
iron moving back and forth over the shining table-
cloth.

" I don't want any little angel with a harp," she said
resolutely, though with a slight hoarseness in her voice.
"I want just my little Ireny standin' on her cricket to
wipe dishes. She wanted to be buried in her red shoes,
and so she was. Some folks thought 'twas a waste,
and that 'twas wrong to indulge her right on the very
brink of eternity. You don't think it was? No more
do I; or them little red shoes would be settin' up
chamber now, along with her little dresses, in the north
closet — two little pink sprigged calicoes and a brown
one for every day hangin' up there now. I washed
'em and ironed 'em and hung 'em away with my own
hands the day after the funeral. But they wasn't
starched, and so they don't look like her when she had
them on. I'll take you up to see them some day along
the last of the week if you happen in, but not of a
Saturday. That's bakin'-day.

" You seem so kind of interested that I've let on the
way Eben Smith does when I give him chores 'round
the house. I never told anybody, not even the minister, all this. When you go along home past the buryin'-
ground, just look over beyond Aunt Rachel's headstone,
and you'll see a little white picket fence, and a marble
slab with a lamb lyin' down on it. It cost me forty-two
dollars and seventy-five cents; and I wouldn't have
begrudged it if it had been fifty dollars in gold. He
lies over on the right hand of where I'm goin' to be
laid. Six years come Thanksgivin' since he passed

away. You won't find any stone, because when I get time to 'tend to it, and find something to my mind, I'm goin' to have a monument for both of us. It won't cost much more than two good stones, and 'twill make a sight more show for the money. Probably they could see it from 'Squire Hopton's. If he'd died when we used to talk it over about livin' with Irene, he'd been a young man. I used to think anybody that lived to be forty had got all the good there was out of this world, and had ought to be ready for the next. Queer, ain't it, that you don't never seem too old to yourself to keep right along!"

Going home we picked our way across the neglected mounds of the old burying-ground, and through tangled grass that shed its seed on us as generously as if we had been good soil, and leaned for a while on the little picket fence that guarded the sleeping child from improper company.

Beneath the white lamb we read: "Irene, aged five years, three months, and two days. For of such is the Kingdom of Heaven."

Then we sat down in the deep grass, and plucked daisies and red clover-heads, and reached them through the fence till the small, tidy mound was quite littered with them; knowing that no little hands could ever place their tribute on it. One of us said, " Poor little Ireny!" and as we sat there till dinner-time talking it over, we indulged fond hopes in an earthly way that in the select society where little Ireny had gone without her mother, hosts of children might be, not suffered, but invited to come and see her; that they might play together in the bright sand on the seashore, and fashion sand pies in celestial scallop shells, and wade in the shining River of Life, and sail boats on its still waters ; that they might wander to pick daisies and weave dandelion chains in the green pastures, shouting their merry songs in chorus till the heavens rang again, and harpers with golden harps should pause to listen to the children's praise ; that at night, with hands full of heavenly trash and white raiment stained with grass and flowers, they might dance along the starlit, dewy way that led to the homes of graver but still tender and gracious older angels, without the shadow of a fear or the faint memory of past reproof to dim the brightness of their happy eyes.

VI

A HOT SUNDAY

It was without doubt a hot Sunday. The angel on the steeple trumpeted persistently towards the south. The great elm between the meeting-house and parsonage drooped its leaves, and not a shiver of breeze lifted them. Even the sheep stopped nibbling the grass-blades they had learned by heart, and lay down in any rag of shade at hand. The horses fastened under the low sheds stamped and whisked in vain. Fly weather had come. Imitation bumble-bees left piles of sawdust in the stalls, and buzzed and worked on the Sabbath Day, grinding out round homestead holes with the accuracy of an auger, and exasperating the overheated fancy of many a restless farm-horse.

The meeting-house door stood wide open, beguiling one to enter with a vain show of coolness. Within, the pulpit rose high and forbidding, a box with two doors set on a pedestal, and approached on either hand by a winding stair patterned to fit a narrow preacher. Tradition asserts that one, Jared Lines, failed to attempt the passage, and preached from the communion-table, finding text and lessons in a pocket Testament, and thus detracting from the remoteness and solemnity of the services. A sermon unaccompanied by thumps on the ancient Bible, which in times of stress was often lifted bodily and dropped on its cushion with much stirring up of dust, was regarded by the elders as a light production, savoring more of worldly learning and display than of spiritual quickening and upbuilding.

The walls of the meeting-house were covered with paper hangings of a mournful character, which represented Pharaoh, a stout figure with muscular arms, again and again on the point of being overwhelmed with his chariots and the horsemen thereof. Wherever the eye turned, it encountered Pharaoh on a brown ground with lighter brown horses and chariots, and a deep-brown thunderous sky overhead. The pattern repeated itself geometrically up, down, and across. It was bewildering to follow the Pharaohs, and quite distracting if one tried also to keep the thread of the sermon.

At the extreme right of the pulpit, there was a break in the figure very restful to the eye, and also to the

fancy, where the paper had failed in length and been
pieced economically with the effect of a rescue, the
upper chariot grappling with the lower, and assisting
the hopeful imagination. Mrs. Elias Hopton told us
that if possible the defect would have been remedied
years ago, because it was bad for the children to get an
idea that Pharaoh might have been saved after all, and
the Providential design made to miscarry. That was
the sentiment, though not here expressed in the words
of our hostess, which had no graphic quality to enable
them to maintain that hold on the mind so essential to
accuracy in quotation.

From the same source we heard with much pleasure
the story of the old minister from Harris, over mountain, who exchanged pulpits one Sunday with Parson
Lum, and gave out the first hymn, beginning with

> "Lord, what a barren land is this,
> That yields us no supply."

Now, Harris had nothing whereof to brag over Hilltop
in point of fertility; and its young farmers were wont
to cast envious eyes at the pumpkins and pound sweet-
ings displayed by the Hilltop youth at the county fair;
a decent sort of jealousy that keeps the country from
stagnation.

Uncle Arad Ridge led the singing in those far-back
days, striking the pitch with his tuning-fork, and loudly
announcing the name of the tune to be sung, while the

congregation rose, and, turning their backs on the minister, faced the choir. Mrs. Hopton, who was quite a girl at the time, though still in pantalets, remembered well the awe she felt when, above the ring of the tuning-fork, the name "Harris," boldly given out, struck the congregation pale. But they joined the choir in singing the good old tune as reverently as possible, fearing lest some judgment should befall the leader for his levity. "And just one year from that time, if you'll believe it," the 'Squire's wife added, "his Ann was laid away in the burying-ground." It was considered the proper thing to stand up for Hilltop, but not to the extent of making light of sacred things on the Sabbath Day.

The momentary coolness of the church as we entered the door was delusive, and an odor of peppermint, combined with the irregular waving of palm-leaf fans, made the air vibrate. Bees buzzed through the open windows, and bumped their heads whenever there was anything to hit, not perceiving that the readiest way out was that by which they came in. The bald-headed spread ample handkerchiefs over their crowns, while foolish younglings dodged and tittered. Outside Bob White called, with no regard for the proprieties, and even walked up and down the hillside in full view of those who owned window sittings. A pair of bobolinks sat close by, he of the black vest and patched coat on the bending tip of a low cedar-bush, while his brown little wife exchanged ideas with him from the ground. By the aid of a key we might have learned all their secrets; but they looked as conscious and secure as two students of Volapük setting out to enjoy themselves. When the black and white coat flew to the next bush, trilling and rolling his melody over and over as he went, the little wife followed silently and perched yards away, while he kept up the conversation.

The bell ceased its melancholy toll as the new candidate walked briskly up the right-hand aisle, dropped a very worldly looking straw hat on the chair beside the communion-table, and mounted fearlessly to his high perch. He looked so painfully young and conscious when his glance swept the audience, that we felt abashed for him and looked the other way, wishing he might have omitted the new moustache, and diverted its effort towards side whiskers. The old minister had died in the winter, and ever since the people had been sorely tried by new-fledged ideas that beat about to no purpose.

But before we had adjusted our minds to judge from appearances whether or no this candidate could be a success, there was a new diversion. A tall young girl came up the left-hand aisle, and with an air of unconsciousness knelt for a moment, the only figure in the four reverse pews. She was what the novelist of to-day is fond of calling a symphony; and the effect was peculiarly cool and refreshing. Beyond the nodding

red roses on high stalks, the tall poppies and chrys-
anthemums, the yellow daisies and carnations, that
bloomed above the rural hats of the Hilltop girls, the
slim figure in pale green, with a pond lily at her belt
and a white sailor hat coiled about with a filmy bit of
illusion, looked like a water-lily herself, sheathed in
coolness.

The young minister foolishly allowed his wandering
glance to be arrested for a moment; then blushed visi-
bly as he turned to the great Bible and failed to find
the place for his text. But we considered that there
would be time enough for that after the opening prayer
and hymn, while the contribution for foreign missions
was being taken up.

Just then an unprovoked breeze slipped in from nowhere in particular, and died out again as soon as it had
performed its mission, whisking off two or three leaves
of the sermon that lay beside the Bible. Mrs. Hopton
pulled the sleeve of her husband, who turned slowly
from his comfortable attitude to ask " What? " and the
two deacons started simultaneously from the same side
of the church, and simultaneously sat down again.
Once more they rose together, with much confusion of
face, in the solemn stillness of the house, when the
young lady, seeing the leaves alight near her own pew,
picked them up carefully and walked with them to the
foot of the pulpit stairs.

The great Rachel in her prime could not have done

the act with more gracious unconsciousness; but the youth who opened the pulpit door that stuck, and came down to receive his papers at her hands, stumbled in his confusion, and the door banged as it saved him from a fall.

"That's the Brumley girl," whispered Mrs. Hopton behind her fan, as she emphasized the fact with one elbow. "Ain't afraid o' nothin', and never was."

After this prelude the sermon turned out but a mild affair, quite in keeping with the sultry weather, though everybody was wide awake at the beginning, and disposed to be critical. But any provocation to deep feeling or unusual stirring up to spiritual effort must have fallen flat on the congregation that day. Fans moved slowly and more slowly, and raked against bonnets and slapped the backs of the next pews, momentarily awaking the sleeper. Mrs. Elias nodded forward as the 'Squire's head fell back, and only the younger portion of the audience were in condition to judge of the sermon, its merits or defects. We decided that the ayes would have it, as happened some weeks later on. For the elders could give no reason why the young man should not be called; and so, after several hearings, they reluctantly yielded to the expressed wish of the younger members, who were growing to have their own way about things in an alarming nineteenth-century fashion.

As we went out after the benediction, leaving the deacons to shake the minister's hand loosely and allow

him the privilege of opening the conversation, our hostess detained us in the vestibule, and beckoned the young
lady from the other aisle.

" Gracie!" she called in a loud whisper. " Come
over here a minute. I want to make you acquainted
with my two young ladies from the city. We think
they're about right. And they're mighty fond of knowing all us country folks."

" Couldn't get a soul to stay with your grandma before, could you? Haven't seen you out to church before
this summer," added Mrs. 'Lias patronizingly. " But
how in this mortal world did you ever do that, Grace?"

" Did I do what?"

" Why, walk right out in meetin' and pick up them
papers! There wa'n't another girl there darst do it to
save her life, hardly. And the men, they all held back
too. My man, he didn't happen to see it in time."

" Why, the young man had to have his sermon, and I
was nearest."

" Well! if 'twas anybody but you, Grace Brumley:
Why, you couldn't have hired me to do it! "

" No, nor me," said Miss Brumley simply. " There
was nothing else to be done, and I didn't stop to think
about it. Why was it any harder than walking into
church, or out of it, or across the green? "

" Well, I can't say," said Mrs. 'Lias with a sigh ; " but
I couldn't have done it no way — no, not for a kingdom."

As Miss Brumley bade us good-morning and walked

away, a little ripple of conversation came in, like the
untoward breeze, from nowhere in particular. Everybody seemed to be talking at once, as in times of politi-
cal excitement.

" Deary me ! " said Aunt Tishy gently, as she raised
her large umbrella. " Did you ever see the beat of it? "

" Brass enough to make a kittle, and sass enough to
fill it ! " piped Uncle Arad, in the high key that deaf
people approve of in others.

" I started to get up some'ers near Brother Biglow,"
said the younger deacon, " but he got ahead of me
twice, and it sorter took all the wind out o' my sails."

" Your sails wa'n't set fur enough to wind'ard, young
man," said Cap'n Saul heartily. "That's what made
'em flop."

The deacon, who was only young by courtesy and a
bachelor to boot, blushed before all the nodding roses
that were coming down the gallery stairs, and turned
aside in some confusion, crushing the brim of his brown
straw hat against 'Squire Hopton's broad shoulders.

The young minister shook hands again with the
elder deacon, and to the relief and disappointment of
every one, accepted our host's invitation to dinner.
He was a nice young fellow, scarcely older than ourselves ; just a boy let loose from the Theological Semi-
nary to try his clipped wings. We had a pleasant
nooning together. It was like entertaining a bright
young freshman, just come to his university with ideas

and good manners, and not yet spoiled by girls or moulded by upper-classmen. He gave us the best he had without any reserves, without one apparent provident thought of laying up good phrases for the next sermon, or memorizing his own fresh ideas. We liked him genuinely, and resolved to say a good word for him whenever we had a chance.

When the early afternoon service was ended, our host proposed hitching up and taking him over mountain before milking-time ; but to his surprise the young man said he preferred to walk, and would wait, if convenient, till evening.

Mrs. Hopton, who stood in wholesome awe of a minister in any stage, explained with much hesitation and choosing of words, that it was not the custom of the house to prepare supper on the day of rest, but that he was welcome to all the bread and milk and cottage cheese he could eat, along with the family. It jarred on her feelings not a little, we could see, to have the minister throw himself down on the grass under the crooked apple-trees as if he had been but a common man, and later on, swing himself by one arm from a bough within jumping distance, to straighten his muscles. But being a reasonable woman she kept these things in her own heart, and did not try to influence her husband's vote when the committee meeting was called in September.

We had our bread and milk under the trees, with no

grace preceding. But the birds sang vespers in a heavenly way, and nobody felt the ceremony less sacred for the omission. The sun was still making prisms of Abner the Second's windows over on Davy's Hill, when our guest picked himself up and bade us a gracious good-by. We had been talking about Abner, and telling our new friend where to find him over mountain. For Abner was spending all his summer days studying for examinations in the hope of entering Yale in the autumn.

The young minister waved us a final farewell from the verge of the common, and we watched his boyish step till the sudden descent of the hill dropped him from sight. In the hollow he appeared again for an instant, like an object seen from the wrong end of a telescope; and Mrs. Hopton, shading her eyes as she looked after him with motherly interest, cried out suddenly: —

"Oh, pa! do go after him as fast as ever you can. He's took the wrong road a'ready."

But the 'Squire, who had just set down two foaming milk-pails, stood on tiptoe, and comprehending the valley in one long look, shook his head knowingly.

"Tain't more'n a couple o' miles further that way, mother, and he'll have to go straight past the Brumleys. I guess she won't let him get lost. Mebbe there'll be a sudden breeze down there, and Grace — she's a master hand at pickin' up the pieces. But I bet Aunt Tishy'll squirm if the parson takes a shine to Grace Brumley. What's the matter of her, you say?"

"Now, pa, hush!" warned Mrs. 'Lias with uncommon vigor and authority. "You and Aunt Tishy and Uncle Arad and all of 'em knows that there ain't a mortal thing the matter of her. She's just as nice a girl as there is anywheres about, only she ain't a bit like the rest of us. That's all there ever was against her, anyway. Her folks died when she was little, and she and grandma live all alone down there. There was a house left 'em and not much else, and folks think Gracie 'd rather read than work. But I don't. Why, she might have kept school. She's smart enough. But Grandma Brumley's losin' her sense, and they say it's a job to take care of her. Gracie can't leave her alone, even of a Sunday.

"They're 'Piscopal. You see how she went down on her knees to say her prayers this morning. She never would talk about herself or anything belongin' to her. But one of the neighbors happened in pretty often, and she found out in some way unbeknown to me that Gracie done fancy-work and sent it to town by the stage-driver. And they do say, but he won't tell what he fetches and carries, that she's took to makin' jellies and such this year. There's sights o' berries all round there. I ain't one to blame a girl for livin' easy whilst she can. It's good to recollect when you're head over ears with a family.

"Abner, now, 's mighty fond of her. That's the pinch with the old folks. They think she's set her cap for him, 'specially since he's goin' to college. You see, when he does marry they want him to get something uncommon. Nobody quite good enough here. Why, some folks will tell you that rosberries from over mountain's ever so much better than ours. Mebbe the soil does make a difference. But folks turn out just about the same wherever you raise 'em."

"They're just about the surest crop there is anywhere," said the 'Squire musing. "You drive over the barrens twenty miles east 'o here, and if they can't raise stuff enough to keep 'em alive skercely, there's no end to the young ones. It's the surest crop there is."

"Well," put in Mrs. 'Lias, "I do hope the minister hasn't got lost. I didn't once think to ask him if he'd got a mother. It's just about as hot since sundown, and I'll go up garret and open the windows. Not a mite of a breeze. But wa'n't it queer the way it started up, not a cloud anywheres, and blew the sermon off! First I thought 'twas a judgment; but now when I turn it over in my mind since he went away, it seems almost as if it might turn out to be a providence. You never know."

"Well, mother," interrupted the 'Squire, "if you've got to guessin' out things, I reckon I'd as good's lock up and go to bed. Sure you shut down that milkroom window? We've got to have some crackin' thunder to keep us awake after a spell like this."

VII

HILLTOP'S DESOLATION

LYING in a hammock day after day, under maple-trees seventy feet high, and looking up at the backs of the leaves overhead, one comes to feel that each leaf is an old friend whose face will greet us when it turns around. There were other trees at the 'Squire's that we loved : ragged locusts catching the filmiest breezes, and turning them over to the maples, — locusts, honey-sweet in flowering time. And there were stunted and crooked apple-trees that blossomed heartily when their time came, making up in sweetness, like many a human being, what nature had denied them of grace. But best of all we loved the maples. Though acres of oaks and chestnuts, beeches and hickories, waved towards the west, just beyond the home meadow, and we could hear from their depths the always unanswered question of the oven-bird as we swung under the nearer shadows, the woodland did not belong to us. The homelier, every-day birds nested in our own two trees, and embraced us in the privacy of their domestic affairs, till we felt that they would miss us quite as much as we

should mourn them, when October came and sent us
back to the dust and racket of the town.

This August day had been intensely, bewilderingly
hot. The air vibrated dizzily, and we felt the weight
of the sky above our heads as if it had been the roof
of an uncertain steamer-berth or the ceiling of an air-
less sleeping-car.
Only here we had
what there was of
freshness and pu-
rity, with no fear
that our modicum
of air had been
thrice breathed before
it reached us. The
cows in the meadow left the
sunny slope where they ate
grass, and thought grass,
and dreamed grass, all the
day long, and walked in sol-
emn, undulatory procession to the little brook corner;
and two cow-buntings followed persistently, darting
and rising, but never far away from their leaders.

The heat grew appalling. Even our comfortable hostess brought out a low rocking-chair and a palm-leaf
fan, and sat down idly in the shade of the nearer maple.
apologizing that this was one of the days when she was
rich enough without work. The bees reproached us

with their busyness; humming-birds dived into the red
trumpets of the great creeper at the porch, fanning
themselves as they complained of their fare.

"Deary me! I guess I could keep to work," sighed
a voice from the rocking-chair, "if I carried two fans
along, the way they do."

By five o'clock the air darkened suddenly, and everything hushed but the crickets. Their "rascally voices"
cut through the silence like knives. Then a great
wind-storm rose as from the earth, swept the streets,
and snatched up the dust from the roadways, to lay it
down as suddenly in the tidy front rooms and halls that
stood open to breathe. Green maple-leaves torn from
the trees flew across our spare room, and flattened themselves on the opposite wall. The curtains strained and
flapped from their moorings, and caught wildly at un-
protected mantel ornaments, dashing them madly into
space, with streams of water and trails of goldenrod
following. The carpet rose in long waves, and tugged
at its fastenings like a ship's canvas. The house rocked
and shuddered, and the chimney dropped two bricks on
the roof to hurry us as we flew up stairs and down,
shutting windows, latching doors, and picking up
pieces. We saw Cap'n Saul reach out a long arm for
a banging shutter; there was a clatter of glass at the
parsonage. "Betty ain't spry enough for a time like
this," gasped Mother Hopton from the garret stairs.
Betty was the old woman who lived all alone in the
deserted parsonage.

"Don't it seem like the end o' the world! There—
I heard it thunder! Now, I do wish 'Lias would come
home.—Why, here he is this blessed minute! You
hadn't ought to run, pa. My! how tired and hot you
be! Drop right down on to the lounge."

"Windows all seen to, mother?"

"Yes, to be sure."

"You ain't hasped the milkroom door?"

"Yes, yes; do set down and get cool."

"Be'n up garret?"

"Why, certain."

"You ain't be'n down cellar?"

"Dear, dear, yes, pa. Be'n down cellar, and hild all
the barrels down," she added with a sense of weakly
humor.

"I bet a cent you didn't rec'lect the woodroom
door."

"Well, there! But that don't matter. I'll go now
and see to it, if only you'll drop down somewheres and
get cool."

"No, you won't; I'll go myself. If you want business done, send a man. Like as not somethin' else'll
be at loose ends; and we're in for a ripper, I tell you!
Heat don't pile up this way for nothin', now."

The storm came tramping on from the northwest,
black above and livid below, bowing the treetops with
shrill whistle and deafening roar. The rain followed
after, hissing as it laid the dust. The first great drops

struck like bullets, punching holes in the roadways.
The lightning quivered incessantly, dancing about the
woodland, shining between the trees, flashing across the
north, lighting up the black world that helplessly
waited and harked. We knew that half Hilltop had
taken refuge in the midst of plump feather beds, and
that the other half sat far from open fireplaces and
doors with its feet on the rungs of chairs, preternat-
urally silent, with an awed hush like that of nature
before the storm burst.

"There goes that old fool of a brindle straight for
the big ellum, and the whole kit and boodle a-fol-
lerin'!" cried the 'Squire, as he shaded his eyes at the
western kitchen window. "And lightnin' always goes
for the likeliest critturs. Hand me down that rubber
coat, mother."

"You ain't a-going to tempt Providence!" cried the
wife in a pitiful, shrill key.

But the 'Squire had no time for a reply. The
heavens opened in one superlative, impossible blaze,
and out of the heart of the blaze came a sound as if the
rocks rent and the mountains fell; as if the foundations
of earth had given way, and chaos was at hand. Each
grasped at the nearest support, blinded by blue flames
that darted everywhere about the room, like bats on a
night when moths are abroad.

The 'Squire was the first to speak. He stood holding
the rubber coat at arm's length, but dropped it and

looked foolish as his wife laid hold of his arm. She had clutched the teakettle in her fright, and stood holding it in one hand while the lid clattered.

"I thought you two was struck," she said, laughing nervously. "You sort of settled right down on to the floor."

"I thought 'twas me," said the 'Squire, "and I ain't quite sure yet. But Lordy! what's afire? Run all of you — somewheres — anywheres! Save something if you can, but run for your lives!"

He caught at a pile of milk-pans ready for the evening's milking, and started for the spare room.

"It's only the church," we gasped, as we reached the windows first and flung open the blinds.

" *Only* the church!" cried the 'Squire, in a passion of grief. "Do you begin to know what that meetin'-house cost? Confound it! Why wa'n't it the 'Piscopal? There goes Cap'n Saul with a couple o' buckets. Wife, get the milk-pails."

A dozen men ran to the pump. Where they came from we could not tell. They were just there, as if the cloud had dropped them too. A line was formed, and pails were passed from hand to hand, but very little water reached the fire. The rain stopped, inconsiderately, as suddenly as it had begun. Flames shot out at the windows of the prim old meeting-house and licked the clapboards dry, creeping and darting toward the steeple. Cap'n Saul capered heavily here and there,

directing, shouting, falling over himself, and lending a
hand everywhere; even venturing to beat in vain at
the doors with an axe. We saw him driven back again
and again. But it was of no use. The heat grew in-
tolerable; and the men stopped work, and stood like
sentinels to guard the houses around. Women with
brooms swept burning cinders from doorsteps and
fences, and put out small blazes that threatened to
kindle the little settlement. The 'Squire hurried home
to say that we must look out for ourselves when the
bell fell. Then he mounted the stairs to guard the
roof. The clouds were passing towards the south, but
a ragged fringe lingered to trickle a few ineffectual
drops on the doomed meeting-house. Uncle Arad
limped across the green to our door, staffing along
with an umbrella, his straw hat set askew, and his long
thin locks dripping on his coat-collar, while Aunt
Tishy, with a woollen shawl over her head, sat down
on the door-sill, a personified grief!

"It's a judgment," she sobbed hoarsely — "a judgment and a solemn warning."

But what was in her mind, or on it, we could not
guess.

Everybody waited — waited as one gathers up the
faculties into one knot when the fuse of a cannon
cracker is lighted, or a man's finger is on the trigger of
a gun. But the flames crawled on, and shot up to the
steeple and played around the bell that hung in loneli-

ness on high, till only the skeleton of the old church
stood with vain bravery defying a paltry enemy.

The timbers were hewn in the old days of honest
work, and stood by each other. But the moment came
when the bell must go, and women held their ears
and pinched their eyelids close, and felt their hearts
stand still with a deadly spasm of pain. The steeple
rocked and the bell tolled one; then down it came
with a dull crash, and buried itself half in the earth.
Showers of sparks and cinders flew to the height of the
steeple — a grand pyrotechnic display for disengaged
eyes. The danger was past; church and steeple, bell
and trumpeting angel, all "in one red ruin blent."
Cap'n Saul volunteered to keep watch all night, so we
knew that Hilltop was safe. He said over and again
that he was just as wide awake as a blackfish, and
might as good 's put it to account. He could turn in
for an hour or two by sun-up, when everybody would
be a-stirring. A dozen or more drenched and muddy
men and women filled the 'Squire's clean kitchen, drink-
ing cider and staying themselves generously from a
milk-pan full of ginger cookies set out on the two-
leaved table, together with great slices of sage cheese
and wedges of apple-pie.

The kettle, restored to its place again, steamed cheerfully; cups and spoons jingled, and the odor of coffee
filled the room. But no amount of good cheer could
stay Hilltop's dreary mourning for its old meeting-
house.

" What shall we do ? " groaned Aunt Tishy, " hymn-books all gone — nothing left but a heap of ashes, and Sunday coming."

" Do ! " exclaimed Uncle Arad, with the force of a sudden inspiration that lifted him from the 'Squire's elbow-chair and set him on his feet, "Clean up the old 'Piscopal ! Guess the Lord won't care, sence we can't help ourselves."

" How can we sing the Lord's songs in a strange land ? " piped the elder deacon, as he helped himself to a second glass of cider.

' Pity if some of us can't remember the old hymn-tunes," said Mrs. Minerva Pease energetically. " The very babes and sucklin's know ' Old Hundred ' and ' Chiny ; ' and betwixt us all we can make shift to keep up the singin' end, if the parson 'll do the rest. There's a sight of work to be done there, though. S'pose we women folks all get together here to-morrow morning with our brooms. 'Squire Hopton 'll let us have pails, I know. And the men, they'll just have to turn in and help move things."

VIII

A NEW FRIEND

Our acquaintance with Miss Brumley, which began at the church porch, developed fast in the few weeks that remained. We were welcomed so heartily when an errand took us one morning to her door — a practical errand in the form of a delicacy from our hostess to the invalid — that we went again and again with increasing zest, as the days began to economize on the evening end. It was of necessity a one-sided affair; for Miss Brumley, with the sole care of an exacting invalid, had scant time for anything outside her own home.

One sunny morning we started with our hostess, who had important business at Harris, which lay in the direction of our favorite walk. The day before 'Squire Hopton had promised to have an order filled for Miss Brumley at " Cap'n Saul's "—an order that had waited long, and increased day by day until somebody happened by.

Country supplies, when one lives at a distance from their source, do not come in like the tides. Their seasons of ebb and flow might well be represented in algebraic formula by x. Two factors in the present problem

were a stray cow and her owner. The 'Squire, after a
luckless chase in the heat of a September afternoon,
glowing and full of wrath, came suddenly upon Miss
Brumley, who opened a hospitable gate and invited him
to come in with her to the cool porch, and refresh himself with raspberry shrub. As the story of his griev-
ance grew to Homeric proportions, his anger cooled,
and his heart, expanding abnormally with the continued
refreshment and sympathy, prompted him to offer any
assistance in his power to the lone women, who kept
neither errand-boy nor horse, and so were liable to the
Biblical embarrassment of empty cruse and barrel.

Immediately upon the 'Squire's return we had the joy
of taking the order to the store, and seeing the leisurely
weighings and measurings develop from shapeless masses
into square-ended parcels, tied with criss-crossings and
bow-knots of brownish twine, which snapped off sharply
against the captain's hard little finger. More than once
it had seemed to us that the scales were not reliable;
the weight-end going up too far every time. When it
came to the precious quarter of Old Hyson tea, we
remonstrated.

"But, Captain Lamb, you made a mistake. It was
only a quarter of a pound."

"Why, bless my eyes, if my hand didn't slip! I'll
be car'ful next time."

Surely the recording angel looked the other way, and
presently turned back a leaf or two to rub out any

dark marks that may have accrued in his youth against the captain's name.

Mrs. Hopton sat between us on the broad seat of the buggy as we set out early the next morning in the direction of Harris, and piloted old Zach skilfully down Meetin'-us Hill, past the ruins of the lamented sacred building, which were matter for shying to the orthodox beast. But our hostess held a firm rein in each hand well up under her chin, and addressed soothing remarks to Zach, who listened with one ear as he made long diagonals down the hill, marking his initial with the wheels all along the damp roadway. The brook at the foot of the hill was at its lowest, so we boldly plunged in with much rocking over stones, to give the beast a drink, and as boldly strained and struggled up the steep bank on the other side. This was also an economic measure, we learned, as the off-wheel tire rattled because it was too dry, and a good soaking in the brook would stop its creak.

At this point our ways diverged, as the road to Harris wound up the hill; so, taking an armful of parcels, we descended from the buggy, and walked along the brookside in the midst of an apology for a country thoroughfare. Grass grew between the ruts, and golden-rod with pale asters blossomed there. On either side the untrimmed bushes made a thick hedge which the spiders laid claim to, spreading their glistening webs with the satisfaction of geometrical professors; looping them from high slender twigs, and fearlessly swinging like mad acrobats, till their gauzy cable caught and gave them a tight-rope for other pranks. Even now, with midsummer in the air, sumacs and swamp maples and blackberry leaves had put on gaudiest colors, defying the fate that already had them in its grasp.

Everything was dewy, sweet, and still. Presently a cricket chirped and then another; and in the distance a meadow-lark, like a rejected lover, sang indefinitely, "You are so-o" —

The cottage we sought stood a little back from the highway, three-quarters hidden by lilacs and rose-

bushes, and a huge trumpet creeper in full scarlet
flower. There was a tangle of honeysuckle at its roots,
unearthly sweet with late, pale blossoms that the bees
were at. A wide porch, over-generous for the country,
held a wicker chair and round table.

As the gate creaked, Miss Brumley, in a pink gingham gown and long white apron, came to the open
door. It was jelly-day, and the odors of a whole summer followed her out into
the cooler air. Our brief
country experience had
taught us the primary
lesson that company is
not needed at crises, and
we hastened to withdraw,
after giving our parcels into
the young girl's hands. But
she urged us so genuinely to
stay, that we lingered, and
at last consented, as we knew

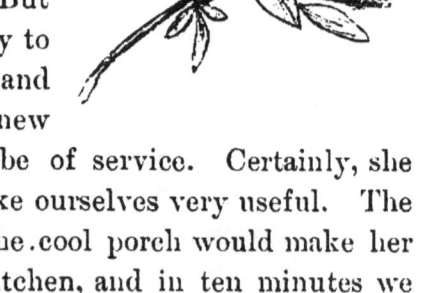

we should if we could be of service. Certainly, she
assured us, we could make ourselves very useful. The
sound of our voices on the cool porch would make her
forget the heat of the kitchen, and in ten minutes we
could help fill the glasses.

Here was another kind of woman from the one we
had dreamed of finding — a woman with the manners
of a princess; a woman, moreover, whose delicate hands

looked as if they had never done anything less graceful
than lute-work in king's palaces.

The long morning was holiday time. Glasses with a
silver spoon to carry off the heat were filled, cooled,
and labelled. The invalid in the bedroom close by was
curious to know what all the talking was about. " You
can't work and talk too," she said severely. " Come
right here, Grace, and tell me who's out there." The in-
terruptions were many and annoying; but our new friend
accepted them, as we found afterwards she accepted
everything that came to her, with a sunny, elastic spirit
and never-failing kindliness.

That day was but the beginning of rare days to lay
up in memory. Sometimes we sat on the porch-steps
and looked over portfolios of sketches. This was the
winter work after berries and fruits were gathered,
canned, and jellied, and made into fragrant jams and
marmalades. Sometimes we posed for our friend when
the artist-cook became the artist-designer; playing a
warming-pan for mandolin in an Eastern balcony scene,
or balancing kitchen crocks on our heads as Greek
maidens with amphoræ. The stern old woman in her
elbow chair looked upon it as a degenerate sort of play
in a working world, where jelly-making brought sure re-
sults. She, too, often posed, though unconsciously, as
Roman matron or Puritan grandam, her resolute features
softened by cap and kerchief that owed their daintiness
to another touch than hers. We, with young enthusi-

asm, hailed the artist so newly discovered, and brought
to her all our books that furnished promising material
for illustration. Already we saw "G. B." writ large
across the glowing future.

Everything about the old house was dainty with
artistic instinct, from the white curtain behind the
kitchen spoons and skimmers, to the scoured floor and
white tables. We must have looked interrogatory; for
Miss Brumley replied to our thoughts, "I don't do
everything. A real old-school gentlewoman comes in
every week and refines things. Haven't you heard of
Aunt Mercy? No? Why, you've missed the best of
Hilltop. Don't think of going away till you have seen
her. Spring cleanings wait for her, and weddings and
funerals would be simply out of the question without
her. She is as angelic in a sick-room as my dear grandmother, who was never happy unless she could comfort
somebody. I often wonder what she has been doing in
heaven all summer.

"But about my house; yes, there is a great deal to
be done, but I am up before the sun, and could do it all
if my hands were not more useful in other ways. It
marks me as over proud, I know." She smiled contentedly, and we knew then that all Hilltop's comment
and censure could not chill nor hinder the even flow in
her veins nor add one drop of bitterness to her cup of
life.

Her own room we longed to carry off in our kodak,

that already held a dozen interiors, and was a constant
surprise to our good neighbors. We thought of our
own room at the 'Squire's, with its green-paper curtains
uneasily rolled up and disagreeable to touch; our two
clean rag mats with vivid colors; our painted chairs
that came off on the backs of our gowns, and held
us when we wished to go; our high bedstead with
pink calico valance, and orange-and-blue quilt above a
mighty feather bed; our tiny pillows edged with home-
knit lace; our narrow looking-glass

that made us wonder what our friends
could see in us to tolerate; and our
wall-paper that we never mentioned.

Here was a little, crooked room,
where the ceiling stooped down to a
four-foot height on one side, and
thrust out a dormer window with
thin muslin curtains full ruffled, and
held back by old-fashioned brass lily knobs and knots
of pale pink ribbon. The oval mirror above a bow
legged low-boy that did duty as toilet-table and chiffo-
nier, was also draped daintily, and gave back one's
casual expression with the precision of a snap shot.
There was a low couch with wide pillows, a white
rug, a round stand with crooked legs, a narrow mantel over a tiny corner fireplace, holding two tall
silver candlesticks with snuffers and tray. Knobbed
brass andirons held birch sticks laid for a fire; books

everywhere, and a pink-lined work-basket added the
last touch of hominess. A frieze of sketches in water-
color ran around the room like a precession of the equi-
noxes. Above the fireplace a snowed-in hamlet with a
rosy glow from the setting sun, a cold thread of moon
above the church spire. Over the east window a mist
of trees, just touched by spring, with a wandering line
of brook among their roots, and a robin with two straws
in his bill planning a nest. Beyond, a garden of scarlet
poppies and a flight of birds; and touching the winter
scene, a glory of goldenrod and cardinal flower with its
feet in a stony brook.

It was all like the magic of a dream, and we dreaded
to see it fade away before our eyes.

One evening we came just after tea, and stayed to be
called for by our host on his way home from church
committee-meeting at the elder deacon's. The grandmother was asleep after a weary day, and peace had
descended upon the lonely little house. The night was
cool, with a foretaste of the coming winter. We were
asked directly up to the little crooked room where the
birch fire was burning softly, with a low moon looking
in at the west window. Miss Brumley sat on the rug
full in the firelight, and we all watched the creeping
flames like devout Parsees. We were thinking of the
summer already closed, and our lost opportunities; and
one said, " To think, we did not know you all these
months! "

Miss Brumley mused a moment.

" To think you do not know Abner Geddie! That is what I have to regret for you. You have lost a great deal out of your lives — and don't know it. I can talk to both of you about him, because you have sense, and don't look on all men as possible lovers. Of course you know Hilltop gossip. So do I. It's untrue, like most gossip, and doesn't reach me. I mean, the real me. Of course it would be annoying if it were worth while; if there weren't better things to think about. After these weeks with you that have put something new into my life, I couldn't in justice let you go away without knowing the one real man in Hilltop. Only I'm afraid I shall fail to make a picture for you. He is working too hard. I asked the young minister about him last Sunday. He always has worked too hard. He always will work too hard. It's in him. You don't mind my telling this to you? Thank you. I wanted you to know that he is a real man; not just stuffed clothes. And he never has to entertain you with his pedigree; just a son of Adam, which was a son of God. Besides, it shows in his eyes. Nothing un-dignifies him. He can teach district school with its babble of noisy young ones, or hoe corn, or hold the plough, feed pigs, or read Plato. Big and little are all one to him. His body does its work well, and so does his mind. They work together like man and angel. A strong team, isn't it? If you meet him in the

potato-patch, he takes off whatever he calls a hat with
as much grace as if it were his Sunday's best; and is
no more affected by his clothes than a scarecrow.

" Aunt Tishy thinks I shall marry him," Miss Brumley laughed softly. " He still has the spirit of a man,"
she added. " When we came here I was a child ten
years old. He was my one real friend in school. They
said I was proud. Very likely. I suppose I did keep
apart from what I didn't like. I must have been a
dreadful little prig. Love of humanity developed
slowly in me, and not very far. Abner looked out for
everything that was stepped on, from a hopper toad to
a dirty youngster with a stubbed toe. I'm afraid I
looked the other way. I was different, they said. But
they were different too. Abner was the only one of
them all that liked me and took my part. I was disagreeable enough to need it all. The big boys made
fun of him, but his loyalty was the enduring kind. I
am four months older than Abner. Everybody thought
I was a great deal older, and I was proud of it. I call
myself four years older now to him when I want to be
motherly. He was really older than I, with a deep experience of trial and unsatisfied ambition that made him
a man long before his time. I look back on those days
with a feeling of motherly pity for the plucky, freckled
little Abner, who was so proud when I, who had been
the taller, had to look up to him, and who took everything hard, from measles to affliction.

"He was one of Dr. Holland's new Adams. The force and genius that were born in him came from another generation, and he made the most of them. I often wonder what he would have been with a father and mother until now. Hampered and limited, I know; never let to do as he chose, any more than his grandfather was before him. They were small souls, that would have fed their eaglet on chicken-meal. Now he has his liberty in a way. Liberty is good for the soul. Otherwise light comes to it through cracks, and stinted. Bars are a great hindrance and make shadows."

She leaned forward to put another stick on the fire, which flashed suddenly in her face and made her beautiful.

"You would love Abner if you knew him. Not as I do, for I know him as nobody else can. I have seen him grow from the ground. Perhaps you think there is a flavor of romance here, but there isn't. If Abner were really dying, I would marry him. But I care too much for his future. I simply stand out of his way and keep shadows from him, my own as well as the others. He will understand it some day better than he does now, dear boy.

"Am I lonely here? Oh, no. When my candle is snuffed out at night I lean across my window-sill and hark to all the small voices in the night-world, till it seems as if each separate little praise belonged to me.

In the city it is different. The tiny, clear notes are confused in the great money-making roar, and the world seems to hurry away from the stars. Here we are always sailing towards them. When we do make port, I wonder if earth will seem as near as they do now.

" My own thoughts keep me busy in new worlds, till sleep shuts the door and makes universal harmony. I need all the daytime cares and perplexities to keep me from being visionary. Sleep-walking in the sunshine is against the law of our own life, which takes care of our bones gratuitously.

" You wonder if I am ever unhappy ? Who can be miserable unless they choose it, with books, and plenty of work, and all one's faculties in good order? I see more than I can think about every hour ; and in some way that I can feel but not explain, everything seems to weave itself into the warp of my life, and make patterns that are pictures to me always."

" I s'pose," said 'Squire Hopton, as tired Zach picked his sleepy way up the hill and stumbled at pebbles, " I s'pose you got all talked out down there 'twas so late. I never could see for the life of me what women folks had to say to each other. They don't go to town meetin' or read the papers. But if I'd been there an' told you what a fight we'd had over the little parson, and how our side come out ahead, you wouldn't have run out o' talk all winter long.

" The brethren voted to give the young feller a clean
four hundred dollars in cash, and the rent o' the parsonage, besides a donation visit in the fall after butcherin'.
The parsonage is worth a good sixty dollars a year.
Then, come spring and fall, our women folks turns out
an' helps clean house and set things to rights, and give
advice. It keeps 'em chirk, and gives 'em something
to talk about for a spell. Ministers' wives — well,
they're a queer lot, take 'em all in all. They don't
take nat'rally to the washtub, but they do like to have
a finger in the pie when it comes to sermons. Sorry
that there ain't a wife here, but then he's got a sister
that's a widow an' no children. Mighty good chance
for her. Ministers' wives ain't gifted in the kitchen-
line, far's I can see ; but I do' know but what their
sisters may be, 'specially if they've been married to
smart business men an' got started straight.

" If I get my guess though, that sister'll have to step
out 'fore long, and let somebody else step in. Understand? I ain't so blind but what I can see through a
ladder yet. An' she'll do better'n most of 'em if she is
different. They all has to be queer some way, an' if
he can put up with it I do' know as we've got any call
to make remarks. The old woman won't help matters
any, but that's their lookout."

IX

THE LAST OF HILLTOP

IT was the evening of our last day at Hilltop, and the western sky was still glowing when we went to bid Uncle Arad and Aunt Tishy good-by. They sat in silence before a dying fire, with Tildy curled up on the braided rug in the warmest place.

"Ef ever I was glad to see a human cretur, it's you two," said Uncle Arad, reaching out a shaky hand, while Aunt Tishy rose to set chairs for us. "Now we've got somebody to talk over things with jest as we did a spell ago," he continued, leaning his head on the staff between his thin knees. "Seems as ef 'twould be a comfort. Did y'ever see the beat o' Abner's up an' dyin' right out o' hand as 'twere?" He winked away a teardrop that glistened on his nose, while Aunt Tishy picked up a corner of her apron.

"Why, that boy jest as good 's belonged to us. All my prop'ty was made over to him. Never brought my mind to bear on a widder. Widder Geddie! Land! The perplexin'ist thing 't ever happened, an' the suddenist. When the parson said he'd took typhoid, thinks to me, the boy's be'n a studyin' too hard. I'll go over an' get hold on him, an' fetch 'im home for a spell. Aunt Tishy's a master hand at boneset tea. When I was down in the mouth once, 'way back in the sixties, old Dr. Buell says he, ' Mis' Ridge, you'd ough' to hev a degree — D. B., says he, doctor o' boneset.' Well, she fetched me through an' saved a big doctor's bill. An' I reckoned 'twould be jest so with Abner.

" So I hitched up an' went over mountain kind o' easy, watchin' the leetle yaller butterflies tiddlin' round, 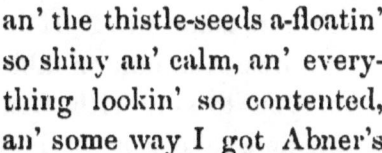 an' the thistle-seeds a-floatin' so shiny an' calm, an' everything lookin' so contented, an' some way I got Abner's life all laid out ahead as easy. Nothin' to hender his bein' a preacher ef he so minded, when he'd got his eddication ; or a lawyer—though it did go a leetle ag'inst the grain ; or a reel good country doctor, drivin' round in his own shay, ownin' land all round his place, layin' up two or three hundred a year mebbe, when we was dead an' gone. I got to sort o' wishin' we could hang on a spell longer 'n we're likely to ; jest curi's to see how things would turn out. An' when I got there moggin' along — 'twas late in the forenoon — he was jest gone ! Married to the Brumley girl, and gone, an' no help for't. Just like snuffin' out a candle accidental. Why, 'tain't reasonable. Here I be, nigh on to ninety year, and he jest in the dew of his youth. We was gettin' so kind o' proud an' set up about 'im — well, the Lord's ways ain't our ways."

"Didn't he look too good to put under ground?" quavered Aunt Tishy. "So like the other Abner! It all came back to me, that he was the boy I used to know so long ago. It didn't seem right to take him into the church, some way. If he could only have been laid on our own communion-table ; but there — it was real good of you to stay with Grandma Brumley and let Grace go and take care of him. They say she just held on those two days and nights, and wouldn't let him die. Seemed as if she lived and breathed for him. Aunt Mercy said she never slept a wink. And when the doctor said he was going, our minister married them jest as solemn as a funeral. They'd sent for him, to please Abner ; for he wouldn't have anybody else, he'd took such a notion to him. Nobody but the doctor and Aunt Mercy for witnesses. They say it was a touching sight."

"The old woman took good care," said Uncle Arad mournfully. "She nussed Abner's mother when she was a-dyin', an' the boy he was dretful nigh to her. I was a-thinkin' jest before you come in, an' a-sayin' to Aunt Tishy, mebbe we've be'n a leetle hard on Grace all along, not thinkin' she set so much store by Abner.

We'd got a notion 'twas the prop'ty, mebbe, along o'
Abner's smartness an' good fam'ly an' all that. I tell
you, human natur's queer stuff — queer stuff. An' I
feel a sight worse to think she won't hev his money,
than I did when I s'posed she was settin' traps for
Abner. Why, his last words to the parson was to let
us know how he'd allays wanted to marry her, sence he
was a boy, so to say, an' she wouldn't. Makes me feel
powerful mean, some way. You see, she's most related
to us, or might 'a' be'n. Her pa was Aunt Rachel's
youngest; that ar Tom Jess took on his knee I told
y' 'bout when you fust come here. The one he said hed
ough' to be'n his'n. Yes, 'twas all wrong, Rachel's
marryin' the way she did. Well, Tom was the likeliest
one on 'em. He was a sight like her. When he got
his freedom suit, he took into his head to go over
mountain an' find somethin' to do. Farmin' allays did
stick in his crop. He pottered round a spell tryin' one
thing an' t'other, an' doin' odd jobs, till jest by a mer-
ackle, as you might say, he got clerk in a book-store an'
married the old man's daughter. He settled down to
bus'ness, steady like, an' bought out the concern when
th' old folks dropped off. He'd be'n mighty glad to
take Aunt Rachel an' do for her, but Mis' Brumley
wouldn't hear to't no way. She's a good deal sot in
her mind yet.

"Well, Tom was car'ful and so was she; an' betwixt
'em they laid up enough to get on comf'table till the

year o' the fever that carried off so many. Then he
died, an' they brought him here to be buried, an' after
a spell his widder sold out an' come here to live with
the little un."

" That's Grace," said Aunt Tishy.

" You see, her folks was all gone, an' she hadn't no
call to go back," continued Uncle Arad. " You didn't
know' s Grace belonged to Aunt Rachel? I wan' to
know ! "

" O Abner, Abner ! " cried Aunt Tishy softly in the
pause. " It does seem as if I couldn't stand it."

" Well, we ain't got to long," said Uncle Arad, with
an eye to comfort. " One day with the Lord's as a
thousan' year."

" That's just the way it seems to me," said Aunt
Tishy, with a nervous catch in her breath very like a
laugh. " It seems a thousand years now since he
passed away."

There was a long silence which the clock improved
with cruel strokes.

" A thousan' years like one day : — a thousan' years
like one day ; " mused Uncle Arad. " 'Twas techin' to
go into that room an' see him a-layin' there so still.
His hand was a holdin' on to Grace's, an' she a-kneelin'
there by the bed. I couldn't help it if I'd died for't.
I bawled like a baby. So I hed to leave. I went out
into the little hallway, an' felt in my coat-tail pockets
an' not a han'kercher there."

"Well!" said Aunt Tishy, rousing and holding on by the chair arms, "you had two clean ones folded up in your breast pocket. I put 'em there myself, for I thought likely's not you'd need 'em. Didn't you get 'round to 'em?"

"Well, no, to tell the truth," said Uncle. Arad meekly. "But I looked into my hat that was a-standin' on a chair, for the red bandanner, an' used it out there. Didn't seem the thing in a house o' mournin'. After a spell they got her to go down-stairs with me, and we hed a talk all alone. Or I guess 'twas me. She was jest like a stun. But that sort's got feelin'. I've seen Aunt Rachel jes' so. Ef you hadn't 'a' known her, you'd thought she didn't care a cookie. I told her we'd reckoned on Abner's doin' well, an' set forth to 'er how we'd left 'im the heft of our prop'ty, 'longside o' what Jess give us, an' now 'twould go to her. I thought she'd be real tickled, an' think mebbe 'twas jest as she'd calc'lated. But the mazin' thing was she said up an' down she wouldn't hev' it. Not uppish you know, but jest sartin in her own mind. 'Twas so sudden I kind o' ketched my breath. She said 't all she wanted was to carry his name long's she lived. And she'd got it. For the rest part she could make her own livin'. That's the gist of her remarks, nigh's I recollect.

"Long in the course o' the day our parson come in ag'in, an' told me more about it. He said how Abner'd

allays felt about marryin' her, only she wouldn't.
She thought he was bound to do somethin' gre't in the
world, an' she wouldn't hender. Then he jest reached
out for her hand — feeble — an' shet his eyes like
goin' to sleep peaceful, an' sithed once — only once.
An' she dropt down on her knees the way she does in
church, holdin' his hand all the time; an' says she
clear an' slow, 'I believe in God the Father A'mighty,
Maker of heaven an' earth.' They all stood around,
the parson an' the doctor an' Aunt Mercy, an' didn't
know what on earth they was agoin' to do. An' then
I come in.

"Nex' day forenoon she made all the arrangements for
the fun'ral an' everything, out of her own head, an'
nobody darst say ay, yes, or no. She told our parson
that night when he set up with him, that all along she'd
felt 'twa'n't fair an' square o' the Lord to make that
boy hev such a tough time, till she didn't know but
what she'd get to be a unbeliever. But now 'twas all
right. She was sartin he'd got somethin' ahead of him
'twas of more account 'n anything he was likely to do
here. Otherways 'twould hev been a sort of a insult to
'im. That's the way it looked to her, y'see. She allays
was queer, a leetle off 's we say, but mebbe no harm in't.
There wa'n't any intended. That I will say, if 'twas
my last words.

"An' there she sot in church that day — the Widder
Geddie — think on't! Jes' like a statoo, in her black

veil an' bunnit; the men a snifflin', an' the women folks
all a cryin' an' takin' on. Thinks to me, · O Absalom,
my son Absalom; O Absalom, my son, my son!
Would God I had died for thee, O Absalom, my son,
my son!' An' when they come to lay 'im 'longside
Aunt Rachel, seems 's if I'd tumble right in too, an' be
done with't. Not much sense in my cumberin' of the
ground an' him gone."

"Did you want to leave me all breathing alone?"
asked Aunt Tishy, a little hurt.

It was dark when we came away and crossed the
green, shuddering unconsciously at the thought of what
lay before us. We had not seen our friend since that
memorable day in church. She had been at Abner's
boarding-house in town, setting his affairs in order.

Of that last interview it is impossible to speak. We
came out into the calm night from an unknown country
remote from time and space. She whom we loved had
great treasure laid up in heaven. She was by far the
richest woman we had ever seen.

As we turned the shadowy corner of the up-hill road,
where only the stars and the brook seemed alive, a
strange figure with waving arms stood directly in our
way. An apparition would not have had power to
startle us there; but it was only Eben Smith, with a
bag of sugar cookies and a big bouquet of fennel.

"Mis' Pease thought you'd reckon of 'em on the

stage," he said, and added, "I'm real pleased to come
acrost you here. Saves me all this tramp up-hill to the
'Square's.''

The morning was still and dewy when the stage
rounded up to the post-office with a warlike toot on the
horn that did not always go off at first. Every one listened, from away beyond the school-house corner and
the sawmill bridge, for the cheerful sound that broke
through the utter silence, like a weekly trumpet call to
something grand and stirring.

We saw Cap'n Saul bring out the mail, two postal
cards and a letter that we had left with him the night
before for company, and that were not urgent. Then
he went back for his coat and climbed up with difficulty,
sitting bareheaded beside the driver. A moment later
he caught his foot and fell over the wheel at our gate,
with his hands full of cinnamon-stick and peppermint
lozenges. Mrs. Hopton hurried out behind us with an
apple-pie carefully tied up in a napkin, which we could
keep, as she had several more; and the 'Squire, not to be
outdone, offered us the "biggest punkin in town."

"If we'd come back next year," he added, "we should
have our choice of a likely couple of lambs or the slip-
p'riest little white pigs you ever see."

We kissed them all round — Mrs. Hopton, Aunt
Tishy, the 'Squire, who blushed like a boy, Uncle Arad,
and Cap'n Saul; while the driver grinned from his high
seat, and made a doubtful remark about feeling or not
feeling safe.

Aunt Tishy said it wasn't likely that we should ever see them all again ; but Uncle Arad braced against the hitching-post, and waved his hat round· and round on the staff held high above his head ; a hilarious farewell that was comforting.

As we dropped below the hill, and lost even the ridge of the world with its shaggy wind-bent trees, the new life in waiting rushed in to fill the vacuum, and Hilltop lay years behind us in the past.